"Don't let them out of your **[sight?]**" Nicole. "I'm serious. They're wild. They **[should?]** be in a cage at the zoo."

Scott turned toward her. "Feel like dancing?" he asked. "We could finish the one we started at the first school dance this year. Remember?"

Remember? Alex thought. Of course she remembered. Unfortunately, it hadn't lasted. . . .

"Let's go." Alex followed Scott back into the living room and out onto the small, makeshift dance floor. If Nicole could just keep an eye on the twins for another thirty minutes, and things with Scott kept going the way they were going, this could end up being one of the best days of Alex's life! The music was pounding, and as she danced, she spun around.

She saw Nicole on the telephone, chatting away.

The twins weren't with her, or anywhere near her.

Alex's happiness quickly turned to enormous fear. Nicole had no idea what she had walked away from.

At that moment Alex knew that for her, the party was over. . . .

The Secret World of Alex Mack™

Alex, You're Glowing!
Bet You Can't!
Bad News Babysitting!
Witch Hunt!
Mistaken Identity!
Cleanup Catastrophe!
Take a Hike!
Go for the Gold!
Poison in Paradise!

Available from MINSTREL Books

the secret world of

ALEX MACK™

Bad News Babysitting!

Ken Lipman

A MINSTREL® BOOK

PUBLISHED BY POCKET BOOKS

New York   London   Toronto   Sydney   Tokyo   Singapore

This book is a work of fiction. Names, characters, places and incidents are products of the author's imagination or are used fictitiously. Any resemblance to actual events or locales or persons, living or dead, is entirely coincidental.

A MINSTREL PAPERBACK *Original*

A Minstrel Book published by
POCKET BOOKS, a division of Simon & Schuster Inc.
1230 Avenue of the Americas, New York, NY 10020

ISBN: 0-671-53446-7

First Minstrel Books printing August 1995

10 9 8 7 6 5

Printed in the U.S.A.

For my mother

CHAPTER 1

Alex Mack sat in English, her final class of the day, doing all she could to ignore her best friend, Raymond Alvarado. Ray had a bad habit of whispering to her as soon as he got bored with the subject matter—which was often.

"You think my dad would let me go bungee jumping?" he asked her quietly.

"No way," she whispered back.

"How about white-water rafting?"

"Of course not," she said.

"Yeah," Ray agreed. "He never lets me do anything."

"Ray, would you please stop talking to me," Alex pleaded.

"Like you really care what Armstrong is saying."

He was right. She listened to Ms. Armstrong rattle on, thinking about how long the last ten minutes of class were going to feel. Though she tried to concentrate, her mind somehow managed to wander back to Scott. She wondered whether she'd run into him in the hallway at the break, whether he'd sit near her at lunch, whether he ever thought about her. She doubted it.

In her heart she knew that she was silly to spend any time at all thinking about him. Except for a couple of brief moments over the school year, she hadn't even had the chance to speak to him. True, he had rescued her from Jessica's insults on the first day of school, and she had danced with him at her first school dance, but even that ended before the song was over. The simple truth was that Scott had Jessica, and Jessica was older, prettier, and cooler in every way than Alex.

Alex's two best girlfriends, Robyn and Nicole, tried to help her through it, but what could they really do for her? She was on her own, and they all knew that having a crush on the most perfect guy in school was only going to lead to disappointment.

"Alexandra?"

Oh, no! Ms. Armstrong wanted an answer from her, and she hadn't been paying attention.

"Yes?" Alex tried to act alert and interested in whatever Ms. Armstrong had been talking about, but her heart started to pound.

"You seemed to be so deep in thought, Alex. The book must have made a great impression on you. I assume, therefore, that you'll have no trouble providing the class with the answer." Alex decided that honesty would be the best policy here.

"What was the question again?" The class giggled at her discomfort. Alex looked at Raymond, hoping that maybe he could help, but he just shrugged at her. He didn't know the answer. She wondered if *he* even knew what the question was.

"The question, Ms. Mack, is why is George forced to take such drastic action against his good friend Lenny at the end of the novel?"

Lenny? George? What was she talking about? Alex opened her mouth but couldn't form any words.

"Maybe I was mistaken, Ms. Mack. Judging from the look on your face, I'd be surprised if you can even tell the class what book we have been discussing for the last twenty minutes."

Alex's head started to spin. She'd been thinking about Scott and talking to Ray for the last twenty

3

minutes. She quickly looked down at the book in front of her.

"Uh . . . *Of Mice and Men?*" Alex answered, but not confidently.

"Yes. *Of Mice and Men.*" Ms. Armstrong seemed disappointed that Alex had gotten the name of the book right. It wasn't much of a victory, Alex knew, but at least it prevented complete humiliation. When the bell rang immediately after, she was saved—at least until the next day.

As she gathered her books and headed out of the room—hoping that Ms. Armstrong would not give her a hard time about her shaky attention span—Raymond came over.

"Thought Armstrong had you nailed for a second there, Alex," he teased.

"Yeah, like *you* knew the answer."

"At least I knew the *question,*" he said with a grin. Alex knew that Ray wasn't any better of a student than she was, so she didn't mind his jokes—usually.

They turned the corner of the hallway to find Robyn and Nicole, headed toward them.

"You girls better talk to Alex," Ray said, shaking his head. "Her schoolwork is just not what it used to be." Raymond smiled and moved on. The girls all headed out together.

"What was Ray talking about?" Nicole asked as they walked across the schoolyard.

"I was thinking about Scott, and Armstrong got me," she explained. "Think he ever thinks about me?"

Nicole and Robyn both made eye contact but said nothing.

"Hey—don't everybody answer at once," Alex said.

"Look, Alex, there's nothing wrong with you liking a guy," Robyn said, "but you did make things harder for yourself by picking a guy who's going out with *her*." The three of them stared at Jessica, who was waiting at the end of the sidewalk, an impatient look on her face. Tall, with dark skin and long thick brown hair, she seemed nineteen, not fourteen. Next to her, Alex felt like a *child*.

"Look at her. She's perfect," cooed Nicole, until Alex shot her a look. "I mean in that really boring, traditional supermodel kind of way. And she is possibly the nastiest girl in school."

"So she's perfect-looking." Alex shrugged. "That's not everything."

"We know," Robyn and Nicole answered.

Alex looked up to see Scott walking past them, on his way to meet Jessica.

He smiled and waved. "Hi, Alex!"

Alex smiled and waved back, and then he was gone, his arm around Jessica. Alex watched them go, feeling just a little more hopeless.

"See? He noticed you," Robyn said. "He didn't have to say hi to you, but he did."

"Robyn's right," Nicole went on. "He definitely likes you. Guys like Scott don't have to say hi to anyone if they don't want. What *you* have to do is stop feeling sorry for yourself and do something about this crush of yours."

"Like what? Should I try to get Jessica transferred to another school?"

"Jessica's not your problem," Nicole assured her. "When it comes to Scott, you're your own worst enemy."

"How can you say that? If a guy has a steady girlfriend, don't you think it's wrong just to ignore her and go after him anyway?" Alex couldn't believe she was actually considering Jessica's feelings—she knew Jessica never considered *hers*.

"Nobody's saying you have to ignore her," Robyn continued. "Just keep in mind how long an average junior high school relationship lasts."

"How long is that?" Alex wondered.

"A few months, tops," Robyn replied.

"Well, Scott and Jessica have been together a lot longer than that," Alex reminded them.

6

"Exactly!" proclaimed Robyn. "Their relationship is bound to end soon!"

Alex both hated and welcomed this kind of talk.
She knew in her heart that even if Jessica didn't
exist, it wouldn't mean that Scott would turn to
her. In fact, there was probably a long waiting list
of cool and beautiful girls in line ahead of her.
"Let's just change the subject, okay?" Alex asked.
"I know you guys are trying to help, but you're
just wasting your time. Scott has no idea how I
feel about him, and if he did, I bet he'd laugh."

Alex glanced up at her friends, and she could
tell by the disappointed look on their faces that
she had taken some of their enthusiasm away from
them. They continued across the street in silence,
until Nicole whirled around and faced Alex, looking furious.

"Why do you always have to do that?" she
demanded.

"Do *what?*"

"Why do you have to put yourself down all the
time? Why would Scott laugh at you? So Jessica's
gorgeous. So what? You have your own special
talents, and you know it!"

Alex was a little surprised at how much her
friends seemed to care about all this. As far as her
"special talents" were concerned, Alex knew she

7

could turn into liquid at will, move objects just by concentrating on them, and send electric bolts from her hands. Alex knew that—but *they* didn't.

"*What* special talents do I have?" she asked them.

Neither Nicole nor Robyn had an answer ready. There was a long and uncomfortable silence, until Robyn blurted:

"Hats! No one has as many hats as you do!"

Alex looked at her closest girlfriends in the whole world. They were smiling broadly at her, trying as hard as they could to encourage her—as if having a lot of hats were a talent! They stopped outside Alex's house.

"You are an incredibly special person, Alex," Nicole told her. "You just have to find a way to show Scott that."

They smiled at her once more, waved, and headed on. Alex opened her front door and wandered inside, wishing she had the same kind of self-confidence that Nicole had.

"Are you stupid or just lazy?" Alex's older sister, Annie, asked as she came down the stairs. Annie was fond of asking Alex questions like that—where either answer was an insult.

"What are you talking about, Annie?"

"The front door. You left it open."

Alex turned to the door, which she had indeed left open. She concentrated on it and, without moving, slammed it shut using her telekinetic power. Alex knew that Annie hated her using her powers at all, especially for little things like closing doors, but sometimes Alex liked to annoy her by doing it anyway.

Annie rolled her eyes as Alex passed her on the way up the stairs, rubbing her hands together for effect, levitating her knapsack alongside her. Annie, frustrated, just shook her head in disgust. Alex continued up the stairs, making the knapsack float along outside the staircase railing.

"Very impressive," Annie said with sarcasm.

"Alex!" Their mother's sudden appearance at the top of the stairs caused Alex to lose her concentration, and the bag fell, crashing down, onto a coffee table below. A china vase on top of it wobbled, then fell to the floor and shattered. Annie had to put her hand over her mouth to keep from bursting out laughing. Barbara Mack rushed past them both to inspect the broken pieces.

"Mom! I'm so sorry!" Alex *was* sorry she had broken the vase, but also relieved that her mom obviously hadn't seen her playing with her powers.

"Your grandmother gave me that vase on my twentieth birthday!" her mother said, very upset.

Alex wasn't exactly sure how old her mother was, but she knew twenty was a long time ago. "Alex, when are you going to learn to be more careful?"

"That's a great question, Mom," Annie added as she headed into the kitchen, leaving her little sister alone and ashamed.

"I didn't mean to, Mom," Alex added weakly, coming downstairs to retrieve her bag. She couldn't bear watching her mother finger the broken pieces, so she bent down to help her.

"Sorry, Mom," Alex repeated.

"It's okay," her mother added, but the tone of her voice said loud and clear that it definitely *wasn't* okay.

Meanwhile, Nicole and Robyn were practically giddy with excitement. Alex's problems with Scott were going to be solved, thanks to them.

"It's already Thursday," Robyn cautioned as they waited for a bus to pass so they could cross the street. "It's pretty short notice to invite everyone to a party Saturday afternoon."

"Come on, Robyn. A party's a party. We could call people on Saturday morning and have a full house a few hours later."

"You sure your mom won't mind?" It was Robyn's job in life to think of every possible thing that could go wrong.

"My parents trust me. Besides, my dad's going to visit his brother on Saturday, and my mom usually has this backlog of work that keeps her busy through most of the weekend. It won't be a problem."

"How will we get Scott there? He barely knows Alex, let alone us. And then there's the Jessica situation."

"We can figure that out later," Nicole assured her. "Come on, let's get to my place and start making calls."

After dinner Alex sat alone in the bedroom that she shared with Annie and looked around at the clutter on her side. It seemed to grow on a daily basis, and also seemed to somehow represent her life—a mess.

She put down *Of Mice and Men*, looked out the window at the town, and thought back to the truck accident which had doused her with an unknown, gold-colored chemical, giving her outrageous powers. Once she had mastered them, with Annie and Ray's help, she thought her life would improve dramatically, and all the things she was struggling with—schoolwork, her genius sister, boys—would suddenly become easier to deal with.

She was wrong. Though the powers were definitely an advantage in certain situations, things that were problems before were still problems—and now she even had the evil Vince, head of security for the Paradise Valley Chemical Plant, searching for her.

Alex sighed. Breaking her mom's vase by accident was typical of the things she accomplished by using her powers. Maybe Annie was right—the powers were best kept secret.

A knock on the door shook her back to reality.

"Come in!"

The door opened, and there stood Robyn and Nicole, grinning from ear to ear. Robyn shut the door, and then both girls excitedly fell onto Alex's bed.

"What are you guys so happy about?" Alex wondered aloud.

"We came so you could thank us face-to-face," Robyn said.

"Thank you for *what?*"

"For providing you with the perfect situation to pursue your future with Scott," Robyn announced. "A party, at Nicole's, on Saturday afternoon. We've already got over fifteen kids who said they'd come, and we just started calling!" Alex's friends could barely contain their joy. They were bouncing up and down on the bed.

"A party? Saturday?"

The girls nodded at the same time.

At first Alex's eyes sparkled at the prospect. But then she sighed and flopped back against her pillow. "Even if Scott came, he'd bring Jessica, so what's the big deal?"

"Stop worrying so much about her!" Robyn cried.

Alex was almost shocked to see Robyn, the one friend she had that was more negative than she was, acting so *hopeful*.

"Aren't you *excited?*" Nicole squealed.

Alex thought about it. If things went well, Alex would finally have the opportunity to approach Scott, talk to him, show him what a special person she really was. The pressure on her would be huge—her friends would expect so much.

Excited? Well, her heart was racing, her mouth felt dry, and her stomach filled with butterflies.

Excited?

Not exactly.

Actually, she was terrified.

CHAPTER 2

Overnight, things changed.

As usual, the alarm went off at seven A.M., but Alex was already awake, lying on her back, looking at the ceiling. She didn't move, letting Annie struggle out of bed to shut it off. Alex hadn't been able to sleep for a while, thinking about the party and Scott. Now, in the bright light of morning, her fear and anxiety about it all was melting away. She felt more relaxed, more confident, and she knew she was very much in debt to Robyn and Nicole, realizing how hard they were working just trying to make her happy.

As Annie lay back down on her bed, trying to

gain a few extra minutes of sleep, Alex popped up, grabbed her bathrobe off the floor, and headed out to the bathroom. She was about to open the door when her father, George—a brilliant but distracted research scientist at the Paradise Valley Chemical Plant—burst out of the bathroom already dressed for work.

"Morning, Alex," he said, passing by her and heading toward the stairs.

"Morning, Dad," she replied. She was about to go in when he stopped, turned around, and called back to her.

"Alex?"

"Yeah, Dad?"

"I just wanted to remind you about the baby-sitting you promised to do for the Watsons."

"Oh . . . right. Okay. I remember."

George smiled at her and hurried down the stairs.

Alex stood in front of the bathroom mirror trying to remember just exactly what he was talking about. . . .

Suddenly it came back to her! Her dad had asked her to sit for his boss's twin sons. Alex, always short of money, had agreed. But when exactly was she supposed to do it? She was sure it wasn't for at least for another week or so, and as long as it wasn't Saturday, she didn't care when it was.

As she splashed water on her face, she wondered why he thought it necessary to remind her so far in advance. Even if it *was* for Saturday, the party was scheduled for the afternoon, and all babysitting happened in the evening. If worst came to worst, she could always babysit after the party. Of course, if things went *really* well with Scott, he might ask her to the movies or something that night and ... She stopped herself. She was definitely getting carried away.

She dried her face with a towel and studied the mirror for any possible blemishes that might have the potential to grow into full-blown pimples by tomorrow's party, but couldn't find any. She played around with her long, straight dark blond hair. *Maybe if I tried—*

"What on earth are you doing in there, Alex?" Annie yelled from the other side of the door, knocking hard three times to make her point.

"Two more minutes, Annie," Alex calmly answered. "I just have to brush my teeth."

"Well, hurry up. Some of us actually care about getting to school on time."

Alex decided not to hurry; it was so rare for her to be the first one into the bathroom, and it was such a position of power between the sisters, that she decided to relax and enjoy it. As she brushed her teeth, she studied herself in the mirror again and actually thought she saw a pretty girl's face. She was feeling confident. This was unusual, and she hoped it would last through the party. Beyond that, she didn't care. Right now the only thing in the world that mattered was that party.

At last she sailed out of the bathroom, smiling serenely as a furious Annie shoved past her. Back in the bedroom, she dressed carefully. After all, Scott would probably see her today at school, and she wanted to look great, hoping to leave him with the best possible impression leading up to Nicole's party. She settled on a plaid jumper, a cotton crocheted hat, and her brand-new black loggerboots. She never felt entirely happy with the way she looked, but this was as close as she ever got. She checked herself out in the full-length mirror one last time and actually felt a slight tingle of excitement as she headed downstairs for breakfast.

All this good feeling sank a little when she entered the kitchen to find her mother trying to glue together the pieces of the broken vase.

"Mom—you fixed it! It looks great," Alex lied. It looked like a smashed vase barely held together by rubber cement. Before her mother could respond, a piece dropped out, and the entire vase fell apart again.

"Thanks, Alex," said her mom, disappointed.

"Maybe I can pay for it with the money I'm going to make babysitting for dad's boss," Alex offered.

"I appreciate the thought, Alex," her mother said, smiling, "but it would take an entire year of babysitting once a week to make up for it. Besides, this vase can't just be replaced. It had real sentimental value to me."

Alex felt awful about it and decided to change the subject. "When *is* that babysitting job, anyway? Do you remember?"

Barbara Mack frowned. "Yes, I do remember. Alex, you have to learn how to write things down and be more organized." She paused to sip her coffee. "It's tomorrow."

"Tomorrow *night*," Alex added hopefully.

"No. Tomorrow afternoon. One o'clock."

Alex's heart sank. It couldn't be.

"Tomorrow afternoon? But I *can't* do it tomorrow afternoon!" Her voice cracked, she was so upset.

"And why might that be?" her mom asked, placing a plate of toasted frozen waffles in front of Alex. She sounded more than a little annoyed.

"I'm . . . I'm going to this party." Alex hated the way it sounded coming out of her mouth, but there it was.

Her mom couldn't contain her anger. "Alex Mack! Your father asked you over three weeks ago if you would do him this small favor, and you agreed to it. Now, on the day before, you suddenly have something else that's more important? A *party*, of all things?"

Alex knew that her mother was completely right, but she couldn't give in so quickly—the party was too important. She could try to explain why to her mom, but she knew it wouldn't work. It would sound selfish and irresponsible—which, of course, it was. Why couldn't she just have remembered the babysitting job? Last night she could have asked Nicole to reschedule the party for Friday or Sunday, but by now it was probably too late.

"Would it be okay if Annie babysat instead of me this one time?" Alex tried timidly.

"Good try, Alex," Annie said with satisfaction as she entered. "Very good. Unfortunately, I already have plans for tomorrow afternoon. What happened, forgot something important again?"

"Yes," Barbara Mack said. "Apparently there's a party that's more important to her than a promise she made to her father."

Alex hated when Annie and her mom joined forces against her—especially when they were right. She looked at the soggy waffles in front of her, realizing that if she'd felt at all hungry before, she sure didn't anymore. She pushed the plate away.

"I'm not hungry, Mom," Alex said.

"Great," Annie said. "I am." She dragged the plate away from Alex and started eating immediately. Alex rose from her chair, wondering how, in the forty minutes since the alarm had gone off, things could have gone from hopeful to depressing so quickly.

"Alex, you have to eat something," her mom urged.

"I'll take an apple with me to school," Alex offered.

"Make sure you eat it," Barbara said, handing her a Granny Smith. Alex looked at it, wondering if she'd ever feel hungry again. As she got to the kitchen door, she turned and gave it one last valiant try.

"Mom? If I could get someone to take my place babysitting tomorrow, would it be okay if I went to the party instead?"

"Alex," her mom answered calmly, "why is this party so important all of a sudden?"

"Yeah," Annie continued. "What's the big deal?"

"It's just that it's Nicole's party, and I promised I'd help her set it up and stuff, and I hate going back on my word and letting her down." *There,* Alex thought, *that sounded reasonable.*

"It's nice to see how concerned you are for your *friend,* Alex," her mother began, sounding icy, "but I'd rather you showed the same kind of consideration for your father. He promised Stan a long time ago that you would look after his boys while he and his wife celebrated their anniversary, and they made their plans accordingly. Don't you think it's right that you live up to your commitment?"

"Yeah, Alex," Annie threw in. "Nobody twisted your arm in the first place."

"Annie, mind your own business," her mother said. Alex was grateful for this small show of support from her mother.

"But if I got someone else—someone smart and trustworthy—do you think the Watsons would really care it wasn't me? I mean, they don't even know me!" Alex was sinking fast, and she knew it.

"No. They know George, and that's good enough for them. It wouldn't make Daddy look very good if you canceled at the last minute, would it?" Barbara was clearly not receptive to the idea of Alex bailing on the job. "Look, I have to get to work," she added. "If you feel that getting someone else to babysit so you can go to the party is the right thing to do, then go right ahead and do it." Barbara Mack then walked to the door, passing Alex on her way out.

"Boy," said Annie, "were those waffles good." Annie then stood and left, too, leaving Alex standing alone, hating this turn of events.

Alex walked to school with Ray, and as he talked, she glanced up at the sky. The clouds were puffy and beautiful against the pure blue background, but Alex was in no mood to appreciate the glories of nature.

"You know, school just gets worse and worse," Ray said. "I'm hearing rumors about *calculus. Calculus,* Alex. I'm only fourteen years old!"

"I know," she repeated lazily. She was thinking about other things. Judging from her mother's attitude, there was no way out of babysitting. Her only hope was to get Nicole to reschedule the party, but here it was Friday morning. Alex was sure that Nicole and Robyn had invited a lot more people and were already heavily into the party preparations.

"Tenth and eleventh grades must be . . . *unspeakable,*" Ray continued, talking mostly to himself.

They walked onto the school grounds, passing Jessica and Scott sitting at a picnic table deep in a private conversation, and suddenly things became clearer for Alex. What difference did it make whether or not she could go to that stupid party? Here she saw Scott almost every single day, had every opportunity to go up and start a conversation with him, yet she never even got close. Either he was with Jessica, like he was now, or she just didn't have the guts to do it. Why would it be any different at a party?

Even if Nicole invited Scott and not Jessica, he would just bring her anyway—it was like they were attached at the hip or something. In a flash Alex felt completely embarrassed—not for having to babysit, but for having been so excited about the party in the first place.

The alarm rang, and slowly the students of Danielle Atron Junior High made their way inside the building. As Alex opened her incredibly messy locker, Nicole raced over, no less bubbly than when she'd shown up at Alex's with Robyn the day before.

"We're only about thirty hours away," she said to Alex, smiling broadly.

"Nicole, you're not going to believe this, but . . ." Alex couldn't continue.

"But *what?*" Nicole said suspiciously,

"I won't be able to make it to the party tomorrow."

"*What?*" Nicole exclaimed, shrieking in a high-pitched voice.

"It's my dad ... I mean, it's me. I promised to babysit for his boss's kids a few weeks ago, and I'd forgotten about it until this morning. And I can't back out. Believe me, I already tried." As Alex finished, she knew she was looking to Nicole for some piece of advice, some brilliant suggestion that would all of a sudden make everything okay. Nicole was by nature a problem solver. She would have the answer.

"You're kidding, right?" was the best Nicole could offer. "Robyn and I have been working non-stop to make this thing happen. It's going to be the party of the decade!"

Alex knew Nicole was exaggerating, but she could see the truth underneath. Everything was going great—except Alex's babysitting obligation.

"Any chance of you changing the party to Sunday afternoon?" Alex asked her.

Nicole looked at her as if she just didn't get it. "We've invited everybody, Alex!" Nicole told her. "There's no way to change it. This party is like a boulder rolling down the side of a mountain. There's no stopping it now."

"You've asked everybody? You even asked *Scott* already?" Alex wondered aloud. Nicole took Alex by the shoulders and turned her so she was facing the other end of the hallway. There, to Alex's surprise, she saw Raymond talking to Scott, having backed him up against his locker.

"Robyn and I thought it was better to have someone else invite him so he couldn't suspect that we were setting it up for you—which, of course, we are. No way he'd know that Ray was working for us. Guys don't do that." She paused, watching the two boys. "Ray's a great friend."

As Nicole spoke, Alex looked over at them: Ray, her best friend since she was old enough to remember, and Scott, someone she hoped would be a major part of her life in the future. She was touched, thinking about how Ray was doing this favor for her. She knew he couldn't understand why she liked Scott so much, since Scott clearly was involved with Jessica, but it didn't matter—he was willing to help her. All her friends were rallying around her, and she was going to end up being stuck all day with two seven-year-old twin boys. She felt like crying . . . or at least whining.

"Alex, you *have* to come. The whole party is for you," Nicole pleaded.

"I know, but what can I do? I asked my mother if I could get a replacement, but she wasn't exactly crazy about that idea."

"Does she know why this party is so important to you?"

"Of course not!" Alex said. She was not ready to talk to her mother about boys. Every time she tried, it ended up getting really embarrassing. Nicole looked concerned, and Alex felt guilty.

"I know how much you're doing for me, Nicole, and I really appreciate it all, but there's nothing I can do. I'm sorry. Besides," she felt it necessary to add, "Scott's in love with Jessica and, party or no party, that's not going to change overnight."

"You have to start somewhere!"

It was true. Alex sighed, feeling helpless. Ray and Scott walked by them, Ray with his arm around Scott, still talking in his ear. As they passed, Ray turned to Alex and Nicole and threw them a wide, toothy grin and a big thumbs-up. It had worked.

Scott was coming to the party.

Alex wasn't.

The bell rang again, and the hallway began to

clear quickly. Nicole leaned over and whispered in her ear as they walked ahead and down the hall.

"We have to figure this out, Alex. I just have a good feeling about this party. I know good things will happen for you there." She rubbed Alex's shoulder and started off, then called back. "By the way—you left your locker open."

Lockers, doors, it was always something. Alex looked at her locker, about twenty feet away. Making sure no one was watching her, she concentrated hard and, using her telekinesis, slammed the locker door shut and closed the lock, spinning the combination. She stood for a moment, risking lateness to feel sorry for herself. Even with her amazing powers, there was no way out of this problem. Right then she knew it. There were no solutions. She wasn't going to the party.

Couldn't she *ever* catch a break?

CHAPTER 3

Alex's family knew to leave her alone on Saturday morning. Sulky and uncommunicative, she spent the early hours sitting in the backyard in a tattered lawn chair. She had no more ideas on how to get out of the babysitting. Even an impassioned phone call the night before from Robyn to Barbara Mack, urging Alex's attendance at the party, failed miserably.

As Alex sat alone, she came to terms with the situation once and for all. It was all her fault—she knew that. *She* had forgotten the babysitting job, no one else. In addition, Raymond had told her that though Scott had agreed to come to the party, he also asked if he could bring someone, and Ray had of course said yes. That meant Jessica would be there, just as Alex had figured from the start, and that would eliminate any chance of her making any headway with Scott. It was better for her to spend a quiet day babysitting, catching up on her schoolwork, finishing *Of Mice and Men*. What would have happened if she *had* been able to go to the party? She could see herself, back against a wall, talking only to Ray, Robyn, and Nicole, looking at Scott all day, never having the nerve to approach him. Yes, it was definitely better that she couldn't go.

She was just starting to doze off when she heard the sound of her father's voice behind her.

"Alex? We're going!"

She turned in the chair and squinted at her parents through the bright sunlight. "So long," she answered unenthusiastically. Barbara and George had decided to spend the day in town, shopping and going to the movies. Her mom claimed that she needed to get George out of the house and away from his laptop computer, but Alex was in such a bad mood that she thought they just wanted to get away from *her*.

"Annie's going to be here with her physics study

group if you have any problems over at the Watsons," her mom offered.

"I think I know how to babysit, Mom," Alex said grumpily.

"Just thought I'd mention it," her mother replied, taking George by the arm and leading him away.

Alex sighed. She and her mom were having a very difficult time communicating. What was Annie's secret? she wondered. She knew what it was: Her mom always gave Annie more space.

Glancing at her watch, Alex saw that it was a quarter after twelve. The Watsons lived about four blocks away, and it would only take her a few minutes to get there, but she also knew there was a stop she'd want to make first. She went back in the house, grabbed her bag, and was about to leave, when she stopped and checked herself out in the mirror. Her baggy jeans and high-top sneakers were good enough for the Watson twins, but . . . you never knew who else you might run into over the course of a day.

She hurried into the bedroom to find Annie lying on the bed, on her stomach, her face in a textbook. Alex began to rapidly change her clothes, and as she did, Annie put the book down and watched her.

"Think the Watson twins won't appreciate your current fashion statement?" she asked teasingly.

"I just felt like changing, all right, Annie? I don't think it's any of your business."

Annie sat up on the edge of the bed as Alex rifled through the closet before she slipped on a red thrift-shop dress, then her black boots, turning in the mirror to evaluate herself.

"Look, Alex," Annie went on, "you don't have to be mad at me just because *you* got stuck sitting."

"Come on, Annie. You had a chance to help me out of this, and you didn't. I mean, a physics study group? *That's* why you couldn't take my place?"

"Alex, you seem to forget that until you were old enough, *I* was the one who had to do all the babysitting. In fact," Annie reminded her, "let's not forget those times I had to babysit *you*."

"How could I forget *those* days, Annie?" Alex replied. "As soon as Mom and Dad would leave, you'd make me shut off the TV and do my homework—even on a Friday. *Worst* babysitter ever."

Annie giggled at that memory, then turned to face Alex seriously. "Now you're all grown up and you can ignore your homework and watch as much TV as you want. Isn't life better?" Alex hated when Annie got sarcastic, which was often. Besides, she didn't watch *that* much TV. "Anyway,"

Annie continued, softening, "this is just a really bad week for me, what with the advanced placement tests on Monday. Otherwise, I would have done it for you."

"Really?" Alex asked.

Annie nodded.

"Well, you still have a chance."

Annie got up from the bed, walked over to Alex, and put her arm around her. "Can't do it, Alex. Sorry." She paused. "After all, I'm sure this is all tied into some major boy-related problem, and I'm aware of what kind of crises they can be."

"Who said anything about boys?" Alex answered defensively.

"We share the same room, Alex. I've heard you on the phone every night with your girlfriends talking about Scott. You're madly in love with him, and he barely knows you exist. Isn't that pretty much it?"

Alex was stung. Whenever Annie got nice, Alex had to be on guard for her cutting attitude to return, because it always did.

"At least I *have* friends, Annie, not study partners." Alex looked back at her sister to make sure that remark had hit hard. It had. "And speaking of sharing the same room, don't you think it's unfair that dad has an office, you have the garage for your lab work, and I'm forced to live in this tiny little room with you?"

Annie looked around at the mess of clothes, magazines, and cassette tapes that littered Alex's side of the room—and cringed. Her side was organized and pristine. "Believe me, Alex, I want you to have your own room. Very much."

Alex looked at the clock. Twelve-twenty. "I gotta go."

"Have fun," Annie said. "If you need my help, don't call."

The activity at Nicole's house was fast and furious as they got ready for the party. She and Robyn had told kids that the party was from one to seven, which meant that most were going to show up closer to three, but Nicole knew there would be some kids arriving early to get the first crack at the food.

Nicole, smart and organized, was putting together bowls of popcorn, platters of sliced fruit and vegetables, and plates of tiny turkey sandwiches. She was a blur, working quickly, hustling from the kitchen to the living room and back again. Though the party was not going to be as interesting without the Alex and Scott angle, she was going to make sure that everyone had a great time anyway.

She'd spent the previous evening making three hours of music tapes. She was prepared and determined to be a great host.

Robyn, on the other hand, wasn't contributing nearly as much. Responsible for the beverages, she was moving slowly and clearly didn't have her mind on what she was doing. A pessimist, Robyn usually foresaw and expected the worst. She thought that was a good policy—if the worst happened, she'd be prepared for it, and if something good happened instead, she'd be pleasantly surprised. The trick was never to get your hopes up. For a change, she had gotten them up over Alex, Scott, and the party, and was feeling very disappointed. Nicole could see this.

"Get over it, Robyn," she said, passing by on her way to the living room with bowls of fat-free cookies.

"How can I?" Robyn shouted after her. "All this work was for Alex, and she can't even be here!"

"Did you ever think that *you* might actually meet someone yourself here? Wouldn't that make it all worthwhile?" Nicole said, returning.

Robyn thought that over briefly, then responded in classic Robyn style. "No way *that's* gonna happen."

"Anyway, it's a long day, and you never know.

34

And I wouldn't write Alex off just yet." They heard a kick on the back door, and Robyn rushed over to open it. Standing there, sweating, a large bag of ice over each shoulder, was Raymond.

"Ray!" Nicole exclaimed. "It's about time!" He dropped the bags to the floor and exhaled.

"Man, those were heavy," he said, then looked at his watch. "It's getting close to one. When's Alex getting here?"

Robyn and Nicole quickly glanced at each other, then just as quickly turned away again, saying nothing.

"Wait, wait, wait . . ." Ray said suspiciously. "What's going on?"

"Alex has a little . . . problem," Nicole said, slicing cheese.

"She's got a lot of problems," Ray replied. "We all do. That's no secret."

"She can't make it," Robyn blurted out.

"*What?*" Ray responded. "I thought we were doing this for *her*. Why didn't you guys tell me she wasn't even going to be here?"

"If we'd told you she wasn't coming, would you have spent your entire morning helping *us?*" Nicole asked.

"No way," he said firmly.

"Exactly," Nicole answered as the doorbell rang.

"There's our first guests. Ray, would you get the door?"

"Why should I? You tricked me into lugging stuff from the deli to here for the last two hours. Why should I help you anymore?" The doorbell rang again, this time with more urgency.

"Please?" Nicole and Robyn asked in unison, smiling sweetly at him.

Ray hesitated before replying. "All *right*," he said, frustrated, walking toward the front door. He stopped and looked back at them. "But you guys owe me *big*." The girls nodded at him with what looked like total sincerity, then, as soon as he was out of the room, giggled and slapped hands.

Alex stood across the street from Nicole's house watching the first group of kids enter. It was almost one o'clock, and she was going to be a little late. She figured a few minutes didn't matter considering how the babysitting was going to be such a setback to her entire life. She saw other groups of partygoers coming down the street, a little more bounce in their steps than usual, and she was jealous. They were all looking forward to an afternoon of fun, food, music, and possible excitement, and Alex was looking at hours of boredom and television with two seven-year-olds.

She had come to Nicole's so she could have a visual image in her mind of what she was going to miss, but now it was time to leave. As she turned around, she almost walked directly into Scott, who had come up behind her. Alex practically gasped upon seeing him.

"Hi, Alex," he said. He was standing next to another boy, maybe a year or two younger, who bore a slight resemblance to him. "This is my cousin Jason from out of town. Jason, this is Alexandra Mack."

"Hi," said Alex, meekly shaking Jason's hand. She loved the way Scott sometimes called her Alexandra. Nobody ever did that except her mother, and then only when she was angry at her.

"So," Alex tried, "going to the party?"

"Yeah," Scott responded. "You?"

"Uh . . . maybe later," Alex stammered, "I mean . . . yeah . . . I just don't know when. . . . I have some stuff I have to do first." She wanted to dig a hole in the ground and climb in—she sounded like such a major idiot!

"Great," Scott replied. "Then I guess we'll see you later. Sounds like it's going to be a major bash." He smiled, then he and Jason crossed the street to Nicole's.

Alex watched them go, then snapped out of it

and hurried off to the Watsons, again resenting her missed opportunity. Scott was there, Jessica hadn't arrived yet, and Alex was leaving. She felt sick.

A brisk walk got her to the Watsons at six minutes after one. Alex rang the bell, and almost immediately the door opened and there stood Stan Watson, George's boss. He looked at Alex, then looked at his watch.

"Sorry I'm late," she offered.

"That's okay," he said, sounding unconvincing. "Come on in."

She entered the house, looking around shyly. The house was not unlike the Mack house, which wasn't surprising—almost every house in Paradise Valley resembled every other one. The Watson house, she could see, was laid out almost identically to hers, except that everything on the left of the Mack house was on the right of the Watsons, and vice versa.

"My wife's almost ready," Stan said. "Maybe I should introduce you to Tad and Tommy." He motioned to the couch where the twins sat next to each other, dressed identically in striped T-shirts, long shorts, and sneakers. They looked adorable and angelic to Alex; they were freshly bathed, their straight blond hair was slick and combed back, and they sat up straight and tall on the couch.

"Hi," Alex said. The boys smiled for a beat but said nothing.

"They're a little shy in front of new people," Stan said.

"How can I tell them apart?" Alex asked.

"It's not easy," he replied. "Tad? Raise your hand for Alex." The boy on the left raised his. "Tommy!" Stan Watson shouted. "I asked Tad to raise *his* hand!" The boy on the left dropped his while the boy on the right raised his. Stan forced a laugh. "They sometimes like to play little games with people."

Who cares? thought Alex. *They've* both *ruined my day.* Since she knew that the real Tad had his hand up, she looked to find something to identify him, and found it—his sneakers had black stripes, and Tommy's had red.

Mrs. Watson came down the stairs, walked up to Alex, and offered her hand. "Hi, Alex. Marian Watson."

"Nice to meet you," Alex said, not exactly being truthful.

"Stan and I will probably be gone until seven this evening."

Great, Alex thought. *Just in time for me to miss the entire party.*

"The twins just had their lunch, so we'll make

them dinner when we get home. In the meantime, they're allowed healthy snacks, but absolutely no cookies or candy. Right, boys?"

The twins nodded vigorously.

"Okay," Alex responded.

"And please don't let them charm you into it. They have very sneaky ways of getting what they want sometimes. We also don't allow any TV during the day, so I hope you brought a book."

"I did," Alex said.

"Well, I guess that's it. I left the number where we'll be on the kitchen table. Feel free to call us if you need to," Mrs. Watson said, leading Stan to the door.

"I'm sure we'll be fine," Alex assured her. "Happy anniversary."

"Thank you," Stan said, smiling. "Your dad is always bragging about you. You're the science whiz, right?"

"No," Alex mumbled. "That's my sister."

"Whatever," he answered. "Either way, I'm sure the boys are in good hands."

"I think they are," Alex said.

"I hope *so*," Mrs. Watson chimed in. She was not smiling.

As soon as the door closed, Alex turned to the couch to face the twins. They were gone.

"Boys?" she called, but heard no response. She walked through the living room and into the dining room, looking for them. "Tad? Tommy?" Hearing noise from the kitchen, she entered to find Tad and Tommy using a chair to climb up onto the kitchen counter so they could raid a large cookie jar on top of the refrigerator. "Please get down from there," Alex said calmly. "You could both get hurt."

"No, we won't. We're good climbers," Tad answered while his brother stuck his hand in the cookie jar. "We do this all the time."

"Your mom said you weren't allowed to have any cookies," Alex said.

"But we're hungry," Tommy answered, sticking a cookie in his mouth. Alex marched up to them and gently tried to pull Tad away, while reaching up to bring Tommy down. As he did, Tad slipped away and ran out of the room, and Tommy slid down the side of the refrigerator to escape, both hands filled with cookies.

In the rush to get away, Tommy shook the refrigerator by accident, causing the glass cookie jar to wobble and fall off. Seeing it head toward the floor, Alex reacted quickly and, using her telekinesis, focused on it, just barely preventing it from crashing to the floor, then guided it safely back to the top. Tommy was gone.

Things were off to a bad start.

"I do *not* have a good feeling about this," Alex muttered to herself as she walked out of the kitchen searching for them.

Following the sound of their footsteps, she went back through the dining room, and as she crossed to the living room, she saw the twins rush up the stairs, giggling.

Alex ran after them, but it was too late. She heard a door slam, then the sound of a loud television booming out from behind it.

Shy around new people? Alex thought. *I don't think so.*

CHAPTER 4

The next hour with the twins made the first ten minutes seem delightful. The two angelic boys on the couch had turned into the wildest kids Alex had ever seen in her life.

After spending five minutes knocking on their locked bedroom door, listening to the loud noise of violence and commercials coming from the TV, she'd had enough. Using her telekinesis, she managed to unlock the door. When she got in, she walked over and shut off the TV. Tad and Tommy moaned in disappointment, then got up and raced out of the room again. She followed, seeing them run into their parents' room and slam *that* door shut. Alex's heart started to beat hard as she went after them—would the whole afternoon be like this? She knew that if she didn't put her foot down soon, she might never get them under control.

She walked quickly down the hall and again used her powers to unlock the door. She burst through the door of the master bedroom to find the twins lying on their parents' bed, smiling and comfortable, watching TV.

"Come on, Alex," Tommy begged. "It's our favorite show."

"Come on, you guys. You know what your mom said about watching TV," Alex tried. She walked over and shut the set off.

"Yeah," Tad said, "but you just don't have to tell her. Please, Alex, please!"

Alex considered this for a moment, but decided against it. "No!" she said firmly.

The boys pouted for a few minutes, kicking their sneakers against the side of their parents' bed. Suddenly Tad's eyes lit up. He whispered in his brother's ear. Tommy grinned.

"We wanna go to Luna Park," he announced.

"I can't take you to an amusement park," Alex said. "First of all, your parents would kill me."

"So?" they both shouted with glee.

44

". . . and second, I don't have any money for us to go to the park with."

"Hey, that's not a problem," said Tad, jumping up from the bed and rushing to the closet.

Tad was in the closet when Alex walked over to see him. His little hand was in his father's pants pocket. To her amazement, he pulled out a wad of bills and held it up triumphantly.

"See?" he said proudly. "Our daddy has lots of money!"

Alex stepped toward him, grabbed the money out of his hand, and shoved it back in the pants.

"What do you think you're doing?" she asked, no longer calm. "We can't just take your father's money."

"But we wanna go to Luna Park!" wailed Tommy, now standing on the bed.

"Please get down from there!" Though she gave it her best voice of authority, it didn't work. He started jumping up and down and was soon joined by Tad, both of them jumping up and down on the bed, singing, laughing, and having a lot of fun.

"We wanna go to Luna Park! We wanna go to Luna Park!" They leaped up and down, up and down, until the bed frame creaked and the floor shook. "We wanna go to Luna Park! We wanna go to Luna Park!" they chanted, laughing very hard.

Alex was shocked. What had happened to those quiet, freshly scrubbed little boys sitting on the couch when she first came in? In the first few hours they had raided the cookie jar, totally ignored their mom's order not to watch TV, tried to steal money from their dad's closet, and were now threatening to destroy their parents' bed. She couldn't let it go on; she wouldn't make it through the afternoon.

The sound of the bed frame cracking made a decision urgent. "We wanna go! We wanna go!" was their now-shortened battle cry. They continued to jump, higher and higher. Their energy was unflagging.

Knowing they weren't watching, Alex concentrated on the foot of the bed and lifted it up a few feet in the air, then let it drop back hard to the floor. The impact sent the twins flying back onto the bed and put a stop to their chanting. For a moment they sat silently, wondering just what exactly had happened. They looked at Alex with suspicion.

"We're not going to Luna Park," Alex told them with finality.

"Then can't we at least go into town?" Tommy asked.

"I don't think so," Alex said firmly. "But maybe if you two behave yourselves for a while, we can talk about it later." The twins looked at each other, disappointed, but said nothing. The truth was that Alex couldn't imagine how she could possibly control them outside of the house—she was having a tough enough time inside. But if she could keep their hopes up, it might keep them calm for a while.

"I don't think your mom and dad would like us in their room," she continued. "Come on, now— let's go back downstairs."

The twins immediately got off the bed and quietly walked out. *Good*, Alex thought. That was more like it. Maybe they were just testing her, since she was a new babysitter, to see what they could get away with. That was only natural. Alex straightened out the bed covers and closed the closet door before following them. For the moment she had gained the upper hand. She just wished she hadn't had to resort to her powers to do it.

In contrast to the troubles at the Watson house, the party at Nicole's could not have been going better. The weather was perfect, the house was filled with kids, the music was jamming, and everyone seemed to be having a great time. Nicole's mom had come down from her office upstairs and had not only given the party her blessing, but had stayed for a while, had something to eat, and even danced with Ray.

"Enjoying yourself, Mom?" Nicole asked her slyly, hinting that it was time for her to head back upstairs and leave the kids alone.

"I'll be going back up in a minute, Nick," she replied, fully aware of what her daughter was trying to tell her. "I just needed a break from my work."

"I understand your need for relaxation, Mom, but you know the effect an adult can have on a party like this. Everyone has a tendency to become a little . . . inhibited."

"Good," her mom said, "let's keep it that way."

As her mom winked and left, Nicole glanced over at the couch where Scott sat next to his cousin chewing popcorn, watching TV, and having a good laugh.

Robyn sidled up next to her. "Did I miss her, or is it possible that Jessica still isn't here yet?"

"No, she isn't," Nicole replied, "but . . . *Oh! Now I get it!*" she gasped.

"Get *what?*" Robyn wondered.

"When Scott asked Ray if he could bring someone, he meant Jason—not Jessica!"

"I'm sure she'll be here eventually," Robyn responded, expecting the worst at all times. Ray walked by, his mouth filled with food.

"There's something weird about these cookies," he said. "They kinda taste like cardboard."

"They're fat-free," Robyn informed him.

"I knew it was something." He started to walk away again when Nicole grabbed his arm, pulling him back abruptly.

"Ray? Could you do us a favor?" she asked.

"I told you guys. My work is done for the day. Whatever you want me to do, you can get someone else to do. I mean," he went on, "I've already danced with your mom."

"And had a great time—I saw you!" Nicole exclaimed.

"True," he admitted.

"Anyway, the favor's not really for me. It's for Alex," Nicole said.

"Alex isn't here," he replied.

"Not yet. I just want you to go talk to Scott and find out whether Jessica's coming or not."

"What am I?" Ray said. "Your designated Scott buddy? I barely know the guy, and it's your party. *You* go ask him."

"See, Ray? That's what worries me about you," Nicole began. "You just don't understand the male-female dynamic at all."

"I guess I don't," he answered proudly.

"Neither do I," Robyn chimed in. "What's a dynamic?"

"I'm talking about the way men and women relate to each other. For example," Nicole continued patiently, "if Robyn or I go up to Scott and start asking questions about Jessica, he'll think that we're either trying to flirt with him or, if he's smart, that we're trying to find out for our friend Alex, which we are. But he can't know that."

"Nicole," Ray said, "what are you talking about?"

"But if *you* go up to him and ask, he'll know it's just some guy thing, and he won't think twice about it."

"Just some guy thing," Ray repeated blankly.

"Yeah," Nicole answered. "Go ask him. It's easier for you."

"Okay," Ray agreed, totally confused by all of Nicole's fast talking.

"And don't be too obvious!" Robyn warned as he headed over.

Ray approached Scott and Jason confidently, dropping himself into a nearby armchair. They were watching a basketball game on TV, the sound muted.

"What's going on?" Ray asked casually.

"Just hanging out," Scott replied. "You meet my cousin Jason yet? Jay, this is Ray. Ray, Jay." All three of them laughed at this, and Ray pressed forward for the information.

"What's this, the Knicks and the Pistons?"

"Yeah," Scott told him. "Second quarter. Knicks are dominating."

"You play some serious ball yourself," Ray said. "Star of the team and all that."

"And I've seen *you* play," Scott replied. "You're good. You should try out for j.v. next year. We could use someone who can hit a jumpshot."

"I don't think so," Ray said. "I can't commit all that time to one thing. I've got to keep my options open. I also play a little saxophone," he bragged.

"Wow!" Jason yelled at the TV, reacting to a missed slam dunk. Ray saw Robyn and Nicole creep up behind them, pretending to be refilling food bowls.

"But maybe I'll consider it," Ray added. "Girls have a thing for ballplayers."

"And ballplayers have a thing for girls," Scott joked. Again, the three of them laughed. Ray chose that moment to go for it.

"Speaking of girls, when's your girlfriend getting here? It's going on three o'clock."

"She's not coming. She's out of town with her

folks until tonight. Jason's disappointed. He's like totally in love with her."

"You're the one who's *married* to her," Jason came back with.

"We're not married," Scott said, "but I gotta admit it sometimes feels like it."

Nicole and Robyn had to do all they could to contain their excitement and to keep from bursting out laughing. "I mean, Jessica's beautiful and all, but sometimes we just don't have anything to talk about."

"Bummer," Jason added with sarcasm.

"Spending all that time with just one person?" Scott said. "It gets tired sometimes." There was a pause in the conversation, and Robyn and Nicole were ready to go, happy to get this glimpse into Scott's not-so-perfect relationship, when he spoke up again. "What's up with that girl Alex?" he asked Ray. "She's not your girlfriend or anything, is she?"

"No," Ray said defensively. "Best friend. We grew up next door to each other. Why? You like her or something?"

"She seems nice," was all Scott said. It was enough for Nicole and Robyn, who dashed to the phone.

*   *   *

They were calling at a bad time. After a brief period of silent Gameboy playing, the twins had somehow managed to recharge themselves, and their crazy energy had returned. They'd spent the last fifteen minutes downstairs running around, chasing each other, and screaming at the top of their lungs. Alex had babysat for some lively kids before, but never any quite this rowdy. And two the same age definitely made it twice as crazy! She was just starting to get fed up when Tommy ran over and snatched her hat off her head.

"Hey—give that back." She was calm at first.

"Come and get it, Alex," Tommy teased, throwing it to his brother.

The phone rang, and Alex didn't know whether to deal with this issue or answer the phone. Of course, it could be the Watsons calling, and if Alex didn't answer, that would be a really big problem.

"I'm going to get the phone," she said, rushing to it, "and I hope it's your mother so I can tell her what little monsters you two are."

The boys just giggled and kept playing Frisbee with her hat.

It wasn't Marian Watson.

"Alex!" Robyn screamed into the phone.

"Robyn, I can't talk now. This is a *really* bad time."

"Alex, you have to come over here! Scott's here, and he's alone! I mean, he's not alone, he's with his cousin, but Jessica's not coming!"

Alex couldn't hear her very well, because Nicole was trying to scream the same thing at the same time. As the girls yelled, the twins fired the hat back and forth across the room to each other.

"I really have to call you back," Alex said, growing increasingly furious.

"You don't get it," Nicole said. "He's asking about *you!* He wants to know if *you're* coming!"

"Get out of here," Alex said, not believing a word, watching the twins. They had wrapped her hat into a ball with a piece of masking tape and were throwing it to each other like a baseball. They were having a great time.

"It's true," Robyn asserted. "He checked with Ray to make sure you weren't going out with him!"

"*What?*" Alex said.

"Yes!" both girls said.

Tommy threw the hat to Tad, who dived, hitting the floor and missing the hat as it sailed across the room. Tad ran to get it.

"I have to go, guys, and there's no point in telling me this anyway, even if it's true. I can't leave."

The twins were on the floor laughing about the hat landing in the fireplace.

"Call us back," Nicole urged. "You need to capitalize on this opportunity."

Alex hung up and stormed over to the twins. "Give me back my hat!" she demanded.

The twins were laughing as if their hat game was the funniest invention since cartoons.

Tad pitched the hat to Tommy.

Tommy ran to the front door and opened it. Then he kicked the hat out the door like a football!

"You are the biggest brats I've ever seen in my life!" Alex yelled. "You just lost any chance you had of going into town, and your parents are going to hear about *everything*."

"Alex! You look funny when you're mad!" Tad said, giggling.

"You better go get your hat," Tommy added, "before a dog gets it!"

Alex shook her head and marched out the front door.

As soon as she bent down to pick it up, she realized what was about to happen.

The front door slammed shut. She heard it being locked.

She ran to the open window, but Tad got there

first. He shut it and locked it. Through the closed window, she could still hear the sound of them laughing, as if it were all just a game. She could try the telekinesis on the window, but couldn't risk the boys seeing her do that.

She was locked out.

CHAPTER 5

Ever since Alex had been drenched by the mysterious chemical off the Paradise Valley Chemical truck, she had been under pressure from Annie not to use the special powers that she had developed. Danielle Atron, the head of the plant, had her entire security force out looking for the unknown kid who'd been doused, and they'd been close to finding Alex more than once.

Both girls knew that if they ever found Alex, they'd probably turn her into an experimental guinea pig or something. She had to be extremely careful not to use the powers in any situation where she could possibly be seen by someone other than Annie and Ray. The plant had offered an enormous reward for anyone who had information about the accident and its "victim," so Alex couldn't trust anyone. To make things even more awkward, she just didn't know how to tell her parents.

The problem with not using the powers was that there were just too many opportunities for her to use them every single day. It was too easy. Today, she'd already used powers to unlock the door and lift up the bed, but otherwise she had restrained herself. But when she was trapped, there was only one thing to do. How could she not?

She always got a little nervous before she liquefied. It was really scary. Nobody, including Annie, could assure her that once she'd turned into liquid she could definitely return to her normal human form. She had changed back every time so far, but she always wondered if the next time it wouldn't happen. The whole experience was exciting and frightening, and Alex knew she shouldn't do it unless there were absolutely no other options available to her. Standing outside the Watson house, with the twins watching and laughing from an upstairs window, she tried to think of one of those options.

She walked to the side of the house, removing

the tape from her hat and putting it firmly back on her head. First she made sure that no window looked down on her. Then she turned back to the street to make sure no pedestrians or cars driving by would see the incredible molecular transformation she was about to go through. She waited for a lazy off-duty taxi to cruise by. When he was gone, she took a deep breath and concentrated.

The first thing she did was relax her mind, to focus, to think about liquid, water, flowing rivers. Once her mind was engaged that way, her body took over. It began to tingle, and she went a little fuzzy, as if she was about to faint. Then there was a flash, almost like a quiet explosion in her body, and suddenly it was as if she was lying face down on the ground. She was, but in liquid form.

Everything Alex did while liquid was a matter of concentration. To move, she would visualize it; her mind propelled her forward. She could see, but not very clearly. She had an awareness of where people and objects were, but she didn't always know who or what they were. She could hear, but the sound was echolike and sometimes unclear. To communicate wasn't easy—she had to concentrate very hard to project her thoughts verbally, and she didn't always know if she was being heard or not. Annie, who had studied all aspects of Alex's liquefying, told her that her liquid voice sounded weird, like a Martian trying to speak English. Alex heard it once on tape and it scared her. The one thing Alex had mastered as liquid was the ability to change shape and size as each situation demanded, especially if it meant trying to avoid being seen.

This time her liquefying had gone quickly and easily, and Alex flattened herself as low as possible in order to slide back into the house under the front door. She had last seen the twins upstairs looking down at her from their bedroom. Assuming they were still up there, she slipped back into the house confidently, but immediately she could hear their footsteps and voices—they were nearby. She scooted under the couch, where she decided to stay to figure out her next move.

As soon as she was underneath, the twins came and sat down on the couch above her. She kept her liquid form and listened to them talk.

"Where do you think she went?" one asked the other.

"I don't know. Maybe she gave up and went home."

"She wouldn't really do that—would she?" The first one said. He sounded a little worried.

"If she leaves us alone for too long, we can try and call Mom. Her dad will probably get fired."

Alex couldn't believe them! They were doing whatever they wanted, and so far, there was little she could do about it. She had to regain control.

Hearing the twins continue their conversation, Alex saw her chance. She slithered out from under the couch and zipped into the kitchen. There, she worked her way into a corner and prepared for the always nerve-racking process of reforming; this, too, required great concentration. As the twins laughed in the background, she had to focus on the image of herself in normal human form—she couldn't be distracted by them, or it wouldn't happen. She saw a picture in her mind of the normal Alex, there was another internal flash, and suddenly she was standing up straight, in the kitchen, feeling a little tired, but *back*.

She wondered what to do next in order to get the twins straightened out. That phone call from Nicole and Robyn had gotten her a little bit excited, but she had to fix things here before she could call back and find out what was really going on. She knew she needed to get the boys under control and put some fear in their hearts first. Of course, she couldn't be sure they even *had* hearts. She walked to the kitchen door, eavesdropping on their conversation.

"It's been like ten minutes. I say we call Mom."

"Yeah. How could she just leave like that?"

Hearing this, Alex softly walked back in toward the couch. The twins' backs were turned so they couldn't see her coming.

"She was way too easy. I like a babysitter who's more of a challenge."

"Well, let's make the call—though Mom's *not* gonna be happy."

"That's okay. She won't get mad at us. She'll blame Alex."

"Will she?" Alex boomed out behind them. They gasped and turned back around. Alex was standing over them, her arms folded, an eyebrow raised. "Surprise, surprise," she said, enjoying the sight of the mouths dropping open.

"Where . . . how did you get in?" Tommy asked.

"You left the kitchen door open," she replied.

"I told you to check that!" Tad grumbled to Tommy.

"I thought I did!" he answered.

"Wasn't there a phone call you boys were about to make?" Alex said, walking to the phone and picking up the receiver. "I'll be happy to dial for you. I'll also be happy to let Mommy and Daddy know everything you two have been up to since they left."

"Come on, Alex," Tommy pleaded. "We were just fooling around. Don't get so mad."

"Then stop fooling around so much," Alex challenged. The boys looked at her, and they blinked first.

"We're sorry," Tad said after a pause. He and his brother then got up and walked upstairs without a peep. Alex could hear them go into their bedroom and close the door. She sat down, exhausted. She wanted to call her friends back, but thought it best to see what the twins' next move would be.

When she didn't hear anything out of them after about fifteen minutes, she thought she was beginning to figure them out. It seemed that each period of out-of-control behavior from them was followed by a period of rest, or, as Alex thought more likely, planning their next move.

Recognizing a break in the action when she saw one, she decided to call the party back to see what all the screaming had been about before. She dialed Nicole's number and waited a long time before someone answered. As the phone rang, Alex checked her watch. Three forty-five. The party was in full swing.

"Hello?" said an unfamiliar voice.

"Is Nicole there?" She had to speak over the

loud party noise in the background. "Tell her it's Alex."

"Hold on," the voice said, and Alex heard the phone drop to the floor. While she waited for Nicole, she listened for sounds of the twins preparing for another assault. She heard nothing.

"Alex?" Nicole said excitedly. "We have a lot to talk about."

For the next few minutes Alex listened while Nicole took her through the complete Scott situation. She repeated word for word, and without exaggeration, the entire conversation between Raymond and Scott. Listening to it, Alex had to admit that it sounded very promising: Jessica was out of town, Scott was basically happy she wasn't there, he had nothing to talk about with her, and he had checked with Ray to make sure he wasn't Alex's boyfriend. By the time Nicole finished, it seemed too good to be true, though Alex knew that sometimes her girlfriends had a tendency to stretch the truth.

"Let's face it," Nicole said in conclusion, "you have to get over here."

"There's no way," Alex responded, "so stop asking. I'm babysitting for the two wildest kids I've ever met, and their parents won't be home until seven. So forget it."

"Bring them over," Nicole suggested.

Alex laughed.

"I'm completely serious!"

"Right," Alex said sarcastically. "It would be very cool for me to show up at your party with two seven-year-old kids. Come on."

"Who has to know? My mom is here. She could watch them for a little while. All you need is an hour with Scott to establish yourself with him. I bet the kids would love to get out of the house."

"Yeah, they definitely would," Alex replied. The idea was tempting, but in her heart Alex knew the whole thing was a bad idea. "There's no way, Nicole," Alex said finally. "I wish I could, but I can't."

"It's the best chance you'll ever have with him. If you don't come, you can't expect our help in the future. We're doing all this for you."

"I know you are. There's just no way."

"If you really wanted to come, you could make it happen." With that, Nicole hung up.

Alex put the phone down. Her mind started racing, and her confidence began to soar. All that time she had spent wondering whether or not Scott ever thought about her—he did! Nicole and Robyn had heard the proof! It was so much easier to talk to someone if you already knew they liked you. Why would Scott ask Ray about her if he didn't? Her first impulse was to call Scott, but she quickly realized how awkward that would be, and how obvious. No, there was only one thing for her to do.

She walked upstairs to the twins' bedroom and knocked on the door.

"What do you want?" Tommy called out in a grumpy voice.

"May I come in?" she asked nicely.

"Nobody's stopping you."

She opened the door to find them both lying on the floor on their stomachs, playing with two armies of toy soldiers. They both looked calm, but neither glanced up at her as she walked in.

"You guys want to take a walk?" she asked.

CHAPTER 6

Instead of the excitement that Alex expected, the twins reacted with suspicion to her suggestion. Though they'd been asking all afternoon for Alex to take them out of the house, her sudden decision obviously made them wonder.

"To where?" Tad asked. "The amusement park?"

"No," Alex said. "Just for a walk."

"Can't we at least go into town? Can't we at least go to the video arcade?" Tommy begged.

"Maybe," she said. "Let's just take it slowly and see whether you two guys can behave yourselves for a while."

Again, the twins looked at each other, but said nothing.

"So . . . are you in?" she asked.

"Definitely," Tommy said.

"Good," Alex told them. "Then pick up your toys and meet me downstairs."

Walking back down, Alex started to wonder whether or not she'd just made a really stupid decision. How could she take the risk of going outside with them where they could run off freely? They were impossible inside—they had almost succeeded in locking her out of the house. She suddenly realized that she had let Nicole and Robyn excite her into making a really bad decision, and she had to change her mind.

She decided to head back upstairs to tell the twins that she'd thought it over and there was no way they were going to go out for a walk. But as she turned, she almost ran into Tad and Tommy standing in front of her, ready to go.

"Okay," Tommy said, "let's go."

"I just realized we can't go," Alex answered. "I . . . I don't have a key to lock up."

Tad reached into his pocket, pulled out a key, and held it up to her. After hesitating, Alex reached over and took it from him.

"All right," she said. "Come on."

They walked toward the door, and when they got there, Alex wheeled around one more time to face them.

"Listen, you guys. Before we leave, I need you to promise me you'll behave."

They said nothing.

"Answer me—can I trust you?"

"Where are we going?" Tommy asked.

"Just for a walk," Alex answered. "What does that have to do with whether I can trust you or not?"

"How come you suddenly want to take a walk?" Tad asked, grinning.

"I thought we could all use a little fresh air."

"Oh. We thought it might be so you could go to some party," Tommy added.

It didn't take Alex long to figure out where they'd gotten their information. They'd been listening in on her conversation with Nicole.

"I can't *believe* you two!" she cried. "Forget it— we're not going." She walked by them and sat down on the couch.

"Come on, Alex," Tad said, almost sweetly. "We were just kidding."

"You listened in on me while I was on the phone!"

"It was an accident," Tommy said innocently. "We're sorry. Please can we go?"

"If you guys do anything out of line, we're coming right back here," she warned.

"Okay!" they said in unison.

Once the three of them stepped outside the house, Alex holding tightly to their hands, she felt a little bit excited again. It was midafternoon, and the weather was gorgeous—sunny, but with a nice, steady breeze. The fresh air felt good, and the twins seemed prepared to behave themselves. There was none of that wild energy in evidence— at least at the moment.

"Which way we going?" Tad asked.

"That way," Alex said, pointing in the direction of Nicole's house.

"But the arcade's *that* way," Tommy replied, pointing the other way.

"Boy, you guys never give up, do you?" They both shook their heads. "We're just going for a walk. Tie your sneaker, Tad."

"I'm Tommy."

"No, you're not," she said firmly. "Now let's go."

They walked in silence for the first few blocks, Alex walking between them, gripping their hands so hard that her wrists hurt. The boys were bouncy and squirmy, trying to pull her this way and that. *It was like trying to walk two frisky puppies!* Alex thought. At one point Tommy slipped out of her grasp and made an attempt to dash away, but Alex held on to Tad with one hand and grabbed Tommy with the other before he could escape.

"Don't do that again," she told them. "I promise you, we'll be back home in a second."

"You're the worst babysitter we've ever had," Tad said with a pout.

"I doubt anybody's ever sat for you more than once. Who would want to?"

"Kids who want their parents to keep their jobs at the chemical plant," Tad yelled.

"Don't be ridiculous," Alex said, trying to remain calm. "What does one thing have to do with the other?"

"Did you ever hear of a man named Eric Michaels?" Tommy asked.

Alex thought for a moment, then realized that the name did ring a bell for her. She remembered her father talking about Eric. He'd been involved in a research project with George, then had been fired unexpectedly in the middle of it.

"He used to work at the plant with my dad," Alex said.

"*Used* to," Tommy emphasized. "His daughter

Tammy sat for us. She wasn't nice to us, either. So our daddy fired her daddy!"

Alex just rolled her eyes and kept walking. *Nonsense!* she thought. Mr. Michaels must have done a bad job at work. He couldn't have gotten fired over his daughter's babysitting . . . could he?

The three of them turned the corner, and Alex found herself in the same spot she had been at earlier, watching kids arrive for the party. From across the street she could see that the party was rocking: Music was blasting out from the house, and through the window Alex could see kids dancing. Though she and the twins were across the street, she could hear the sounds of laughter and loud voices.

"Here we are at the party," Tad said.

"I knew it," his brother added.

"Just wait a second," Alex said.

The boys stamped their feet and squirmed, looking impatient.

As she stood and looked at Nicole's house, Alex suddenly felt pangs of fear again. The idea of her actually going in with the twins, finding Scott, going up to him, and connecting with him on some meaningful level just seemed impossible to her now that she was there. Nicole and Robyn had probably exaggerated his interest in her, and they would both be expecting way too much from the situation.

At the very best, the experience would be disappointing. At the worst, it would be completely humiliating. Alex would end up leaving the party knowing that Scott didn't care at all about her, and all her dreams would be shattered. Her girlfriends, in their effort to help her, were actually luring her into a trap.

She didn't have the guts to go through with it.

Alex decided at that moment that she would rather have her dreams of someday being with Scott—no matter how unrealistic—than the harsh reality that she had no chance. If she didn't try, she couldn't fail. She didn't want to lose the little hope she had, and she knew that going to the party would accomplish just that. No, the right thing to do was to turn around, walk away, and forget all about Scott and the party.

"Let's get out of here!" Tad whined.

"Okay," Alex said. "Come on." They turned and started off in the other direction.

"Alex! Is that *you*?"

Alex and the twins turned back to see a very excited Nicole coming out of the house. She ran across the street to them.

Seeing Nicole, and afraid that she would give

away Alex's real intentions, Alex spoke first. "Hi, Nicole," she said calmly. "We decided to take a walk, and we ended up here."

"Fibber!" Tad said.

"You knew where you were taking us all along," Tommy added.

"I'm really glad you did," Nicole responded. She turned and smiled flirtatiously at the twins. "And who are these two handsome boys?"

Alex had to check their sneakers once again. "This is Tad, and this is Tommy."

Nicole smiled broadly and held out her hand to them. "I'm Nicole," she said. They shook her hand, still suspicious, but quickly being won over by Nicole's charm. "How old are you guys? Eleven?" They loved that.

"We're seven," Tommy said shyly.

"Wow," Nicole said. "You're really big for your age, aren't you? This party's for kids twelve and up, but I won't tell anyone if you don't."

"We really should go back," Alex said, meaning it. She was getting butterflies in her stomach.

"Oh, come *on!*" Tad cried. "Aren't you gonna let us have *any* fun?"

Nicole looked up at Alex, smiling slyly. It was working.

"Yeah, Alex," she continued. "Just come in for a little while? I'll take care of these guys."

"All right," Alex said, amazed at how quickly Nicole had manipulated them. "Just for a few minutes." She held out their hands to Nicole as they crossed the street.

"Oh, they don't want to come in holding my hand," Nicole said. "Do you?"

The twins both shook their heads.

Nicole opened the front door, and the raucous sounds of the party blasted out. As soon as they were inside, Alex's eyes darted about, looking for Scott. At first she couldn't see him.

"Guys?" Nicole said to the twins. "There's lots of food in the backyard. Go help yourselves. I'll be right there."

"Cool," Tommy said, and the boys headed straight for the back.

Alex turned to Nicole. "I thought you said your mom would watch them."

"I know," Nicole answered, "but she's upstairs working and I don't want to bother her. I'll stay with them."

"Don't let them out of your sight," Alex told her. "I'm serious. They're wild. They should be in a cage at the zoo."

"I think they're cute," Nicole said. "Anyway, didn't I tame them pretty quickly?"

"It won't last," Alex warned. "Get out there and keep an eye on them."

"Alex, trust me. I know what I'm doing."

"Be careful, Nicole."

"Scott's around here somewhere," Nicole said, ignoring her. "Good luck." She squeezed Alex's hand.

As Nicole let go, Alex waded into a sea of familiar faces, almost instantly forgetting about the twins. She trusted Nicole completely, and, for a few minutes at least, she had more important things to worry about. She moved through couples dancing, saying hello to her friends, her eyes peeled.

Ten feet in front of her, she saw Scott enter the kitchen. Her heart felt like it dropped three feet straight down.

Robyn passed by him, saw Alex, and threw her arms around her excitedly. "I can't believe you made it!" she screamed.

"I'm just gonna be here for a few minutes," Alex said, looking over Robyn's shoulder and toward the kitchen.

"I just saw the twins," Robyn said. "They're really cute."

"Don't make me gag," Alex said. "Is Nicole watching them?"

"They'll be fine," Robyn assured her. "It's time for you to do what you have to do."

Alex nodded and walked toward the kitchen.

When she entered, the room was empty except for Scott, who was leaning against the sink, drinking a tall glass of water, his eyes closed, his head back. If she wanted to, she could have turned around and gone back out, and he never would have known she'd been there.

Instead, she stepped forward.

Scott finished his water, put the glass in the sink, then turned toward her.

"Hi!" he said, smiling.

He really seems happy to see me! Alex thought.

"Hi," was the best response she could come up with at the moment, but she could tell right away that she didn't feel as nervous as she thought she would. She assumed she was simply numb.

They looked at each other but said nothing, and it felt awkward. They then both spoke—at the same time.

"I'm sorry," Alex said after they'd stopped. "What were you saying?"

"I just asked why you were getting here so late."

"Because my parents stuck me babysitting today," she said.

"Oh."

"Actually, that's not really true. I agreed to do it a few weeks ago."

"And you're finished now?" he asked.

"Not really," she said, giggling. "I brought the two kids over here."

"Really?" he said, laughing. "Great idea! You get paid for watching them, *and* you get to go to the party!"

"I shouldn't stay too long," Alex said. "You wouldn't believe these kids. They're monsters. Twins. Seven years old."

"I wasn't exactly an angel at seven myself," Scott said. "Let's see 'em."

"Okay," she answered, "as long as I don't have to talk to them. If I have a half hour away from them, I want to enjoy it."

"You're only staying a half hour?" he asked. He seemed disappointed!

"Well, you know," she replied vaguely. "We'll see how it goes." They walked to the back door, and Scott opened it. Standing in the doorway, Alex look out onto the sea of kids in the backyard, looking for the twins.

"They're they are," Scott said. "Meek as little

lambs." Alex looked over and, to her surprise and delight, saw them sitting cross-legged on the lawn in front of Nicole. All three were laughing and seemed to be having a great time. Nicole had them totally under control. *She is such a good friend,* Alex thought.

"I guess Nicole is good with kids," Alex explained.

"Or maybe you're not," Scott said, teasing.

"That's probably true," Alex admitted. "Let's get out of here before they see me and turn into animals again."

They came back into the kitchen, and Alex felt great. She was totally comfortable with Scott, and he was hanging out with her. True, it had only been a couple of minutes, but she was off to a great start. This was all she wanted—to be with him in a relaxed, unpressured environment, away from school, away from Jessica.

Even spending just these few minutes with him, she knew why she liked him. He wasn't like a lot of the other boys in school. He was cute, but it wasn't just that. He was a star athlete, but it wasn't that, either—he never even brought up sports unless you did. He was just easy to be with. He was nice, friendly, and respectful of other people.

Alex had recently heard her mom use a word

that she thought was a perfect description of Scott, and why she liked him so much. *Unpretentious.* That's what he was. He didn't pretend to be anything but what he was. He was comfortable just being himself, something Alex really wanted to be.

"Feel like dancing a little?" he asked her. "We could finish the one we started at the first school dance this year. Remember?"

Remember? Alex thought. Of course she remembered. It was the only time, before this, that she really got a chance to get close to him. Unfortunately, it hadn't lasted.

"Yeah, I remember," she said. "Jessica sort of cut in. I thought she was gonna kill me."

"There's nothing to worry about now," Scott said. "Jessica's not here."

"She's not?" Alex said, faking innocence.

"Nope."

"Then let's go." Alex followed Scott back into the living room and out onto the small, makeshift dance floor. She couldn't think of the last time she had felt this happy. Nicole and Robyn were heroic for having arranged this entire party just for her, and it was working out perfectly. If Nicole could just keep an eye on the twins for another thirty minutes, and things with Scott kept going the way they were going, this could end up being one of the best days of Alex's life.

The music was pounding, and Alex was dancing, relaxed and joyous. As she danced, she spun around.

She saw Nicole on the telephone, chatting away.

The twins weren't with her, or anywhere near her.

Alex's happiness quickly turned to enormous fear. Nicole had no idea what she had walked away from.

At that moment Alex knew that for her, the party was over.

CHAPTER 7

Fortunately for Alex, the song ended quickly. She could at least claim to have finished one dance with Scott, even though the rest of her life was about to end.

"Where are you going?" Scott asked as she drifted off the dance floor and toward Nicole.

"Be right back," Alex said, even though she knew she wouldn't. She got to Nicole, who was obviously in the process of trying to get someone else to the party.

"No, it'll be going on for hours," she was saying. "You should definitely get over here."

"Nicole," Alex said, trying to interrupt.

"Just a sec, Alex. . . . Oh, Rick? Hurry up. We'll see you soon." She hung up the phone and smiled at Alex. "I was watching you," she said. "You're doing *great*."

"Nicole, where are the twins?" Alex asked. She tried to keep her fear and desperation hidden, but she failed.

"Relax, relax . . . I just left them with Robyn. They're fine."

"*Robyn?*" Alex yelled. "They'll eat Robyn *alive!*"

"No, they won't," Nicole said. "They're really sweet. You should just give them a chance."

"Where were they when you left them?" Alex asked. "In the backyard?

"Yes, but—" Nicole couldn't finish her sentence before Alex was dragging her back there.

As they left the kitchen, Alex bumped into Robyn, who was being followed by Jason. No twins. "Alex!" Robyn said and tried to hug her again.

Alex pushed her away. "Robyn, where are the twins?"

"Jason asked me to dance, so I left them with Ray," Robyn told her. "Besides, they hated me anyway. What a couple of brats."

Even Nicole could sense the trouble that was developing. "Robyn, I told *you* to watch them!" she said, her voice rising.

"What's the big deal?" Robyn asked innocently. "Go on out there. I'm sure you guys are worried over nothing."

Alex and Nicole rushed out.

They burst through the back door into the yard, looking for Ray, or better yet, the twins.

"There he is!" Nicole exclaimed. They ran over to Ray, who was building an enormous sandwich at the picnic table.

"Hey, guys," Ray said happily. "Glad you could make it, Al. Doesn't Nicole throw an awesome party?"

"Where are the twins?" Alex yelled.

"Calm down, calm down. They're over . . ." Ray turned to the far side of the yard, looking for them.

"Where?" Nicole urged.

"They *were* there," Raymond answered timidly.

Alex rushed over to where Ray was pointing, Nicole following. She saw no sign of Tad or Tommy, just a bunch of teenagers drinking soda and leaning against the wall.

"Did you guys see any twins around here?" Alex asked them.

"You mean the next-door neighbors?" a girl with dyed red hair responded.

"No," Alex said, "Two seven-year-old boys. Twins. They came with me."

"Oh," the redhead said. "I just figured they were from next door, 'cause they climbed over the wall a minute ago. I thought they were just going back home."

Alex and Nicole ran to the wall and looked over into the neighbor's yard. Empty. Not a twin in sight.

"Oh, *no!*" Alex shouted, then turned to Nicole.

"Who lives there?" she asked.

"The Ruckers," Nicole said. "They're away for the weekend."

"I'm dead!" Alex said. She ran back to the house, heading for the front door. She plowed right into the living room, straight through the dance floor, momentarily separating Robyn from Jason. She ignored all the questions and shouts of surprise.

When she got out onto the sidewalk, she felt like crying. The twins weren't in the Ruckers' front yard, either. In fact, there was no one in sight. She ran into the middle of the street, then had to jump back as a car honked and swerved a little to avoid her.

"Watch where you're going, you stupid kid!" the driver yelled.

I am a stupid kid, Alex thought, looking both

ways and seeing noting in either direction. *I am the stupidest, most selfish kid in the entire world—and boy, am I going to pay for it!* Wherever they were going, the twins had gotten a huge head start on her. She had no idea what to do in order to find them.

She walked back to the sidewalk and sat down on the steps of Nicole's house, clutching her head in her hands. She sat that way for what seemed like hours, but it was really only a couple of minutes.

"Alex?" It was Nicole's voice.

Alex looked up to see Nicole and Robyn standing in front of her.

"They're gone," Alex said, stating the obvious. "You promised to watch them."

"I know," Nicole said. "It's my fault. I'm so sorry."

"No, it's my fault," Robyn offered.

"No, it's mine," Alex echoed. "I never should have come here. I never should have listened to you guys." Hearing footsteps behind her, Alex turned to see Scott, Jason, and Ray approaching. She couldn't have been more embarrassed.

"What's up?" Scott asked.

"The twins," Alex said. "They escaped."

The four of them started talking at once, while Alex sat on the ground, trying to organize her thoughts. What were her options? If she called the police, or the Watsons, her life would be ruined. Her father would almost certainly lose his job, and she would be grounded . . . for years, probably. Maybe for the rest of her life! No matter what she did, she was in deep, deep trouble. She could only hope that they were safe. "We have to go look for them," she said to the others.

"Who's *we?*" asked Ray.

"As many of you as I can get," Alex replied. "And please—let's keep this a secret for now. While you decide who's coming with me, I have a phone call to make." She stood up and walked back into the house, suddenly filled with more determination than fear. If she was going to go down, she was not going to go down without a fight.

The party was still going strong. Kids were still laughing, eating, dancing, having a great time, totally unaware of the huge hole that Alex had put herself in. She walked into the kitchen, picked up the phone, and dialed. After four long rings, someone finally picked up.

"Hello?" Annie said.

"Hi, Annie. It's me."

"We're studying, Alex. What do you want?"

"I need you," Alex began.

"How unusual," Annie countered sarcastically. "What is it this time? And don't even ask me to come relieve you so you can go to your party. There's no way."

"It's a lot more serious than that," Alex said. "And please don't get mad at me. Just help me." Alex's voice broke a little, and she knew Annie noticed.

"I'm listening," Annie said calmly.

"I lost the twins."

Annie laughed. "You *what?*"

"It's not funny," Alex said. "I took a walk with them, and they ran away. They're the biggest brats you've ever seen, but now they're gone and I don't know what to do. If I don't find them, Dad's definitely gonna get fired."

"Where are you?" Annie asked, sounding very concerned.

"Nicole's," Alex answered, feeling humiliated.

"Oh, *Alex!*" Annie replied. The disappointment in her voice made Alex feel even worse.

"I know," she said, accepting the blame.

"Stay right there," Annie said. "I'm on my way."

Alex hung up the phone just as Nicole's mother entered. Alex didn't feel like talking to anyone at the moment, especially an adult, but there was no way out of it.

"Hi, Ms. Wilson," Alex said.

"Alexandra Mack! How *are* you?" She walked

over to Alex and gave her a big hug. Receiving this show of love from Nicole's mom just made her feel more guilty. She wondered if she'd get such a nice response if she knew how selfish and irresponsible Alex really was.

"I'm fine," Alex lied.

"I thought Nicole told me you couldn't come, that you had to babysit or something."

"I finished early," Alex said. *Earlier than I should have*, she thought.

"Seems like a great party," Ms. Wilson said, "though I've been trying to work through it. It's not easy with all the noise. I'm sure you kids don't mind me staying upstairs."

"I wish you could have been down here for the whole thing," Alex told her. *The twins never would have gotten away from* you.

"What a nice thing to say, Alex."

Suddenly the music booming in the living room stopped abruptly, midsong. They then heard Nicole's voice in the living room.

"Everyone, listen up!"

Alex and Nicole's mom drifted out to see what was going on. They got to the living room to see the petite Nicole standing on a chair, addressing the entire party in a strong voice.

"Due to some unforeseen circumstances, the

party is going to have to end immediately." Everyone in the entire house seemed to groan at once. "I know we've all had a great time," she continued, "but I have to ask you to all leave now! Thanks for coming, and we'll see you at the next one!"

Ms. Wilson looked at Alex. Alex shrugged. Nicole approached.

"The party's over?" her mom said.

"Yup," Nicole said.

"May I ask why?"

"We ran out of ice."

"You ran out of ice?" her mom repeated.

"Yes," Nicole said.

"Is everything all right here, Nicole?"

"Yes, Mom," Nicole replied calmly, "everything's fine."

Her mom looked at her questioningly, then just nodded and headed back upstairs.

The party emptied out in a hurry, leaving only Alex, Nicole, Robyn, and Ray. Alex had hoped that Scott would stay, but wasn't surprised when he didn't. She had exposed herself as the measly seventh grader she was, immature and unable even to babysit properly. Though she had totally enjoyed her time with Scott, all that success had gone down the drain, and the day was ending up a horrible disaster.

"I say we just call the police and put this problem in their hands," Ray was saying when Annie burst through the door.

"I've got a friend with a minivan outside," she said. "Who's coming on the search?"

"We all are," Robyn answered.

"Then let's get moving," Annie said, and they all filed out. Annie waited for Alex and put her arm around her. "Scared?" she asked her younger sister.

"Yes," Alex replied.

"We'll find them," Annie said. "We'll figure a way out." Those words meant a lot to Alex.

They climbed into the van. Behind the wheel was an eleventh grader named Chris, who Alex knew from the frequent study sessions he had with Annie at their house. Alex thought that Annie might actually have a crush on him, but of course she would never admit it. At this moment Alex was just glad that her sister knew someone old enough to drive.

When they were all seated, Annie in the front next to Chris, she turned to Alex for direction.

"All right. Where do you think they could have gone?" she asked.

"I'm almost positive they went into town," Alex replied. "They were begging me to take them to the video arcade."

"That's our first stop," Annie told Chris, and he started the ignition. He had driven about fifty feet when Nicole yelled out:

"Stop the van!"

The van stopped short, and Alex turned to see Scott racing up alongside. He stuck his head in the window on Annie's side.

"Need one more?" he asked. Annie threw Alex a quick glance, and Nicole nudged her. She couldn't believe they thought, at this moment, that she cared.

"The more the merrier," Annie said. "Climb in."

Ray opened the door and Scott got in. Nicole deftly moved out of the seat she was in next to Alex so it the only one available to him. Alex couldn't believe it. Even in a time of crisis like this, Nicole was trying to fix them up! As soon as Scott put his seat belt on, the van took off again. Alex looked at Annie, who mouthed "Happy now?" to her.

"About how long has it been since they got away?" Annie asked.

Ray looked at his watch. "Almost twenty minutes."

"They got a good head start on us," she said. "Everybody, keep your eyes out the window at all times. Maybe one of us will see them—or at least some kind of clue."

The van drove through the streets of Paradise Valley and toward the center of town. They passed the Watson house, and Alex looked longingly at it, thinking of how none of this would have happened if they'd just stayed there. But as her dad always said, that was like locking the barn door after the horse had already run away.

Everyone was quiet, their eyes peeled for the twins. Scott leaned over to Alex. "After I walked Jason home, I thought I'd come back and help you guys out," he said. "I feel it was kind of my fault. I was distracting you when they got away."

"I appreciate you taking the blame," Alex replied, "but believe me, it's totally *my* fault. Thanks for coming back." She smiled at him, and he smiled back. Unfortunately, Annie saw the whole thing.

"Do you two want to keep your eyes out for the twins, or would you rather just . . ." As Annie paused, Alex winced, expecting a stinging remark from her sister. "Just keep your eyes out," was all she said. Alex owed her one.

"We're getting close to town," Chris announced. "Anyone know how to get to the video arcade?"

"I do," Ray answered, leaning forward. "Make a left here, then a right. It'll be across the street." As they neared it, Alex could only hope she had guessed right. If they didn't find the kids soon, they would have to call the police.

"There it is," Ray said.

Chris maneuvered the van into a parking space nearby. Everyone got ready to get out, but Alex spoke up.

"I better go in alone," she said. "If they see all of us coming, who knows what they'll do?" She stood up and moved toward the door, squeezing past Scott.

"We'll get them," he said. "It's Paradise Valley. Where could they go?" He patted her shoulder in support. It felt good.

She got out of the van and walked into the arcade, which was crowded on this Saturday afternoon. Alex had never been a big fan of video games, and the loud explosions and computer voices generated from the machines, combined with the screams of the mostly male players, gave her an instant headache. She walked over to an old, thin man on the phone, an unlit cigar in his mouth, who seemed to be in charge. She was about to speak to him when he screamed into the phone.

"I'm *not* kidding!" he yelled. "It's gonna cost me plenty!" Alex looked around as she waited for him to get off. No sign of Tad and Tommy. "Yeah? Well, get over here as soon as you can!" the man said. Then he slammed down the receiver and walked away. Alex hurried after him.

"Sir?" she said quietly.

"I don't have time, kid," he answered. "You can go get change from Mrs. Gulden over there!"

"I just wanted to ask you if you've seen two little blond twin boys come in here within the last half hour or so."

The fury with which the man stopped and looked at her frightened Alex.

"Who are *you?*" he asked, fuming.

"I'm . . . I'm a friend of their parents," she said.

"Yeah? Well, you can tell their parents that they owe me some *cash!*"

"What did they do?" she asked.

"What did they *do?*" he repeated. "How's *this?*" He led Alex over to a corner and jabbed his cigar at a huge video game. On top of it a giant soda cup lay on its side. Soda was spilled all over the machine, running into the cracks and down over the controls. One of the knobs had come off, and there was a quarter jammed in the coin slot. "Those brats jammed my Doomslayer Two machine. My best game—out of commission! Then they took off!"

"How long ago?"

"I don't know ... five minutes maybe?"

Alex turned and bolted out of the store, the angry voice of the man ringing in her ears.

"Hey! Get back here!" he yelled. "I need their names!"

But she didn't stop. She ran back out into the street. Looking both ways, she took a guess and headed to her right, running down the block. Hearing the loud roar of a city bus starting up alongside her, Alex stopped and had to turn away from the heavy black exhaust fumes that it emitted. As it pulled away, Alex looked up in time to see the faces of Tad and Tommy pressed against the back window, grinning and waving.

The bus picked up steam. Alex chased after it.

"Hey, wait! Stop!" she yelled to the driver.

But the driver ignored her and kept going. She fell back, and the bus rumbled ahead. *They're getting away!* Alex was fast and did all she could to keep up, hoping to catch it by the next stop. She ran harder than she'd ever run before, harder even than when she ran on the track at school. The bus seemed to be getting away, but then in the distance she saw it slow down for the next stop.

She was going to catch it.

As she got closer, totally out of breath, she saw Tad and Tommy escaping out of the back door. They ran ahead down the street and around the corner. Alex ran after them, but her lungs were hurting, and there was no way she could catch up to them. They pulled away and were gone.

She turned around and ran the three blocks back to the waiting minivan and her friends. The door opened and Alex climbed in, wheezing.

"What's up?" Annie asked.

"I just saw them," Alex said, "but they got away again."

"Which way did they go?" Nicole said.

"Down the block and around the corner."

"Where do you think they're going?" Scott wondered.

"I know where they're going," Alex said. "They're going to the amusement park."

CHAPTER 8

Despite having been so close to them, it wasn't long before Alex and her friends had fallen way behind again. The minivan had only gotten a couple of blocks when they were suddenly caught in something rare for Paradise Valley: a traffic jam. A car in the middle of the street had stalled, and suddenly no one was moving. Chris and other drivers were getting impatient, and horns were honking. Alex was extremely frustrated—the twins had escaped again.

"Ray," Alex said, "how far is the amusement park from here?"

"Fifteen minutes walking, maybe five driving," he answered, "once we get started."

"They've already had a nice head start," Annie said, "and it doesn't look as if we're going to get moving for another few minutes."

"What makes you think they're going to the amusement park?" Robyn asked. "The amusement park is expensive. Where would two little kids get that kind of money?"

Alex thought back to the incident with their father's pants. "They have their ways," she replied.

"Oh, no," Chris said. "The tow truck can't even get through. We'll never get off this street."

Alex knew time was running out. "We can't wait here," she said. "A few of us have to go ahead on foot. Annie, you, me, and Ray should get going. As soon as traffic clears, you guys meet us there."

Annie and Ray both knew why Alex had picked them—there was a chance that she might have to use her powers, and they were the only ones who could be witness to them. "The rest of you guys meet us at Luna Park at the main gate—and make sure we have the exit covered so they can't get away again. Annie? Ray? Let's go."

Robyn opened the door to the minivan.

"Go get 'em!" Scott yelled. Ray, Annie and Alex jumped out and started running as fast as they could.

Ray was a very speedy runner and knew where

he was going, so he broke into the lead. It looked as if Alex and Annie couldn't stay with him, but knowing what was at stake for Alex if they couldn't nab the twins, they managed to stay close behind. Alex was still winded from before, but managed to keep up. Ray even knew some short-cuts, through yards, into parking lots and over fences, and it wasn't long before they could see the tall rides of Luna Park in the distance. Alex and Annie were doing some serious huffing and puffing.

"I hope you're right about where they're going," Annie said with difficulty.

"I am," Alex replied.

"It's Saturday. Gonna be really crowded there. Gonna be hard to find them." Annie was breathing heavily; track and field was definitely not *her* specialty.

"Have another idea, Annie?" asked Alex. "Even if we find them, I'll probably be grounded for life as it is."

"Should I care?"

"Yes," Alex said. "Every minute that I'm not at school, I'll be home. In our room ... playing loud music ... getting in your way ... annoying you."

"All right—made your point," Annie said.

They got to the main gate of the park and found

themselves on the end of a long line waiting to get in. "You guys wait in line," Ray said. "I'll see if the twins are up in front." He went up ahead while Alex and Annie struggled to catch their breath.

"Alex," Annie began, "how could you *possibly* have taken the twins to the party?"

"Look, Annie, you don't have to rub it in. I know how stupid it was. Of course, what kind of kids do you think would actually climb a fence to escape?"

"From you?" Annie said. "Smart kids."

Ray came back to them with his thumb in the air. "Alex was right," he said. "The guy at the gate said twins went in a few minutes ago."

"Don't you have to be at least twelve or something to get in without an adult?" Annie asked.

"Yeah. They went in with an adult, some lady," Ray said. "Probably just asked someone to take them in."

"Probably *paid* someone," Alex said.

"Speaking of money," Ray added. "You realize it's fifteen bucks admission here?"

Alex and Annie immediately reached into their pockets. Would it be possible the twins could afford to get in, but they couldn't? "I've only got three dollars," Alex said.

"I've got nothing," said Annie.

Ray smiled and pulled a wad of money out of

his shorts. "Good thing I forgot to give Nicole's mom her change back for the party stuff I bought. Of course, you guys are gonna have to find a way to pay her back." He paused. "Today," he added.

Alex looked at Annie, pleading. She knew Annie had some money at home from a recent science fair she'd won, but Alex also knew Annie was saving it for a powerful new laptop computer. "Please," Alex said.

"Okay," Annie said. "But we're gonna have to work something out."

"Maybe we could explain we were just looking for somebody, and they'd let us in for free," Alex suggested.

Annie rolled her eyes. "Give me a break, Alex. They'd just think we were trying to get in for free."

"I'll pay interest on it."

"You sure will," Annie informed her.

The line moved fairly quickly, and soon the three of them were inside the huge, bustling park. Annie was right; it was packed with kids and families, and the prospect of finding the two little kids amidst it all seemed almost impossible.

"We only have about two hours of sunlight left," Annie warned. "Once it gets dark, our chances of finding them are going to be much worse."

"We need to split up, each taking a different

area," Alex suggested. They walked ahead to a large map of the park.

"I'll take the area from the Outer Limits ride to the Wild West Extravaganza," Annie said, pointing. "Alex, you take from the Thunderstorm Roller Coaster to the Prehistoric Park. Ray, you take from the Evil Dungeon to the food court."

"All *right!*" he said.

"No eating or going on rides," Alex said, causing his excitement to disappear. "We don't have any time to waste."

"If any of us finds the twins, grab them and hold them tight," Annie said. "Get help from a security guard if you have to. We'll meet back here at the map every hour on the hour. Got that?" Alex and Ray nodded.

"Let's get these brats," Ray said.

As Alex started off toward her area, Annie grabbed her.

"You know what I'm going to say, don't you?" she said.

"I think so," Alex replied.

"Don't—under any circumstances—use your powers here. The park is jammed with people. If anybody sees you, you could end up in more trouble than you already are."

"I doubt that," Alex said.

"Be careful, Alex. I'm warning you."

Alex walked through the crowd toward her section of the park. She looked around and couldn't believe the enormous task that faced them. And even if they *did* manage to find the twins, would that save her now?

All the boys had to do was take their parents through the actual events of the day in order to bury her. She could of course tell them all the stuff the kids had done in the house, but that stuff would pale compared to her own misdeeds. After all, she was in junior high school—she was supposed to know better. Though the kids had run away, it would seem as if she had lost them. And why? Because she had wanted to go to a party to talk to some boy. How could she have been so irresponsible?

Alex looked at the faces of what seemed like hundreds of kids walking by. Just when she again thought about how impossible it would be to find them, she found them.

They were standing about thirty feet in front of her, stuffing their pudgy little faces with cotton candy.

"Tad! Tommy!" she yelled. As soon as she did, she knew she shouldn't have. Hearing her, and seeing her struggle to get through the crowd to them, they ran.

She did her best to follow them. She was at first relieved to see that they were safe, but then quickly changed her mind and wanted to kill them. At one point she had a clear view of Tommy and was tempted to throw a magnetic force field or something at him, but there were too many people around, and Annie had warned her. The twins were laughing as they ran, so even though Alex yelled out, "Somebody grab those kids!" people thought they were just playing, and nobody moved a muscle to help her. The twins were shifty and quick, and each seemed to know where the other was going. They raced ahead, and Alex did everything she could to keep them in her sights, but it wasn't easy.

When the twins ran into an empty area behind some rest rooms, Alex saw an opportunity. She had fallen about twenty feet behind and was losing them. She looked around. Good! Nobody was watching. Alex used her telekinesis to pull the lace on Tad's sneaker, untying it. It was enough to trip Tad and send him to the ground.

"Tommy!" he cried. "Wait up."

Tommy stopped, then ran back to help him to his feet. As he bent down, Alex got closer, and as they were about to get up and start running again, she threw herself at their legs, tackling them both.

"Got you!" she cried triumphantly, holding on tightly to both of them as they all lay sprawled on the ground.

"What's this?" The three of them looked up to see a uniformed security guard staring down at them.

"It's okay, sir. Everything's under control—" Alex began, but was quickly interrupted by both of the twins, who started crying.

"This girl's been chasing after us all day, trying to take our money!" Tommy yelled, looking sweet and sad at the same time.

"Wait just a second," Alex said calmly.

"It's true!" Tad said. "She won't stop bothering us! We don't even *know* her!"

"Listen, sir, I can explain," Alex replied while the twins wailed in the background. "I'm responsible for these two, and—"

"First of all, get off them," the security guard said. Alex stood up, as did the twins. They were now crying and clinging to the legs of the guard. Even Alex was impressed by their acting. "Now," said the guard, "who are *you?*"

"My name's Alex Mack. I'm babysitting for these two boys."

"That's not *true!*" Tad yelled. "She's lying! We've never seen her before!"

"She just wants our money!" Tommy wailed.

Alex groaned. She couldn't believe they were doing this!

"You're babysitting for them?" the guard asked.

"Yes," Alex answered, trying to stay calm.

"You brought them here?"

"Well, not exactly. They ran away from me and came here by themselves."

"They ran away from you?" the guard said, looking skeptical. "What kind of babysitter are you?"

"A lousy one," she admitted. The guard turned to the twins, who were still crying and holding on to him.

"There, there," the guard said, patting their shoulders. "Now, who brought you fellas into the park?"

"I did." A lady drifted over, a hot dog in one hand, a huge soda in the other.

"Mommy!" the twins yelled and ran over to her.

"What?" Alex cried. "She's not their mother!"

"I am so," the woman said, handing the guard tickets. "Here's their admission stubs. They came with me and my husband. Who's *this?*" She pointed to Alex.

"She's trying to rob us!" Tad yelled.

"Do I look like a thief?" Alex said to the guard. "I don't who this woman is, but—"

"These are your boys?" the guard asked the lady as she continued eating.

"They are. Todd and Timmy. Our pride and joy."

"Please keep an eye on them, ma'am. There are some very scary people around these days," the guard said, glaring at Alex.

"I won't let them out of my sight," she promised. She put her arms around the twins, and the three of them walked away.

Alex was in total disbelief.

The guard looked down at her and clucked his tongue. "Now, missy, what am I gonna do with *you?*" he asked Alex.

She didn't know what to say. She was tired of fighting. He wasn't going to believe her no matter what she said. "That's not their mother," she tried, but even she knew it sounded unconvincing.

"Yeah? Sounds to me as if you have quite an imagination."

"No," Alex said, *"they* do."

"Tell you what," the guard said. "I'll let this one slide. But you stay away from those kids." As he led Alex away, she looked over her shoulder in time to see Tommy handing the woman some money. She started to tell the guard, but changed her mind. There was no way he was going to believe her anyway.

After they were a good hundred feet from where Alex had tackled the twins, the guard took his hand off her shoulder.

"If I see you anywhere near those kids, you're outta here," he warned her.

"Yes, sir," she replied weakly.

As soon as he headed off in another direction and was out of sight, she turned and headed back, frightened. On her way she passed the woman, who was counting her money.

"You're a liar," Alex said to her.

"Honey, we all lie sometimes," the woman replied with a shrug. "I bet you've lied a whole bunch of times today already."

Alex blushed. She couldn't dispute that. She walked on, then suddenly stopped and checked her pockets. Finding the three bucks, she ran back to the woman.

"Listen," she said, holding out the money, "I have only these three dollars on me. But if you can tell me where the twins went, it's yours."

The woman looked her over, then smiled. "You got some nerve," she said. "What do you take me for?"

Alex looked at the lady without blinking. "Somebody who'll do anything for money?"

The woman smiled and ripped the three bucks out of Alex's hand. "I left them at the Harrison House," she said.

"Thanks," Alex said and grabbed the three bucks right back. "See you later."

"Hey!" the woman yelled, but Alex was gone.

She walked quickly to the Harrison Haunted House, which was known throughout Paradise Valley as possibly the scariest haunted house in the entire world. Rumor had it that in the 1940s, the house had been owned by Cecilia and Alfred Harrison, a very old, very strange, reclusive couple.

The Harrisons never left the house, never allowed anyone into it, and threatened to kill anyone who tried. The town, however, wanted to build a highway that would run straight through the plot that their house stood on. The town sent warning after warning that the Harrisons would have to evacuate their house or have the local police come get them, but the warnings were ignored.

Finally a day before construction of the highway was scheduled to begin, two local sheriffs came to get them out. They entered the house to find Cecilia and Alfred facedown at the dinner table, dead.

As the sheriffs inspected the bodies, a huge chandelier fell down from above, killing both sheriffs instantly. Convinced that the house was haunted, the town decided to reroute the highway, leaving the Harrison house alone.

Now, people said, the Harrisons lived in the house as ghosts, still trying to keep people away from it. Alex, like everybody else in town, had heard the story of the Harrisons and shrugged it off as just another ghost story. The founders of Luna Park, however, saw the profit in opening up such a notorious place to the public and built the entire park around it. It was still the park's most popular attraction.

As Alex approached it, she saw Tad and Tommy at the end of the line, wiggling and squirming, waiting to get in. She walked up to them quietly, put her hands on their necks and squeezed gently.

"We're going home," she said.

"Not so fast," said the security guard.

CHAPTER 9

Alex was being marched through the crowd by the guard, and it seemed like everyone in the park was stopping and staring at her. What a way for her to top off the day—busted for something she hadn't even done! She knew that she would eventually be able to clear herself of whatever wrongdoing the guard thought she was guilty of, but by then the damage would be done.

She looked at her watch—it was almost time for her to meet back up with Annie and Ray. Too bad she was being hustled off to the Luna Park security station.

"I warned you and you just ignored me," the

guard said. "Now you're gonna pay the price." He led her into a small bungalow where another security guard sat, his feet up on a desk, fast asleep. "Jerry!" the guard yelled, waking him. "Wake up. We got a live one here, a real troublemaker. A two-time loser."

"What'd she do, Mikey?" Jerry asked.

"Disobeyed instructions of a park officer," he answered to Alex's shock.

"But I'm the *babysitter!*" she replied.

"When I want you to talk, I'll ask you, okay? For now, just sit down and be quiet." Alex hated being bossed around by some guy who was acting like a real police officer but wasn't. There were guards like him at school. Tin soldiers, Ray called them. Square badges.

She sat on a hard wooden chair and looked out the window at the hundreds of people outside having fun. Now that she was under some sort of Luna Park arrest, she could definitely say that this had turned into the worst day of her life.

"Where are your parents?" Mike asked.

"At the movies," Alex answered.

"What theater?"

"Don't know."

"What's your phone number?"

"555-5785." Alex couldn't make up a fake number; she just didn't have it in her. Besides, it would just make things worse. When Mike started dialing, she wished she had.

"I'm gonna leave a message, let 'em know just what their little girl's been up to," he said. Alex couldn't let that happen. Her heart pounded as she waited for someone to answer. "Machine," he said. Thinking quickly, Alex's eyes followed the phone cord to the wall, focusing on the jack. She waited for Mike to start talking.

"Yes, uh, Mr. Mack? This is Mike Slivowitz, calling from Luna Park . . ."

Using her power, Alex managed to pull the plug out of the wall, disconnecting the call.

Mike was oblivious. ". . . we have your daughter Alex at our security station here. She's been causing some trouble at the park today. Please call us when you get in so we can take care of this matter. 555-7447. Thank you."

As he hung up, Alex used telekinesis to plug the phone back in. Mike had no idea what she'd done, and her parents would have no idea what he wanted them to hear. She knew, however, that she couldn't hold things off much longer.

She had to act. Time was running out.

Mike opened the door. "I'm going back out to finish my watch, Jerry. *Jerry!*"

Jerry had fallen back asleep. Mike's shout woke him up again. "What did ya say, Mikey?"

"I said I'm going back out again. Keep an eye on this kid. If her parents call, walkie me."

"You got it," Jerry said. Alex could see that Jerry was the worst security guard imaginable.

As Mike left, Alex smiled at him. He didn't respond, just picked up his chair and moved it in front of the door, blocking it. In less than ten seconds he closed his eyes, dropped his chin to his chest, and fell back asleep. Alex waited, then tried his name.

"Jerry?"

He mumbled, but didn't really answer.

Again she waited. "Jerry!" she said, louder.

Nothing. He was out.

She stood up, closed her eyes, and shut her mind down again. She thought of the ocean, of waves pounding the surf. In a flash she was a puddle on the floor. She slithered toward the window, climbed up the wall, and back out into the park.

Having reached freedom, she went behind some bushes and reformed again. For a moment she thought of picking up Ray and Annie. But she decided she didn't really have the time and took off toward the Harrison House again. She could only hope that Tad and Tommy would still be there.

Alex had been in the house years before as a little girl and had come away unimpressed. It was just an old run-down house filled with furniture from the 1940s, using some cheesy special effects like phony recorded voices of the Harrisons and some supposedly scary clues of their past. If Alex hadn't been scared of it then, she knew the twins wouldn't be now.

She had to change that.

When she got to the house, there was a line forming for the next tour. She approached a woman up front, who was handing out tickets.

"Is there a tour going on right now?" Alex asked.

"Yes," the woman replied.

"How much longer is it going to last?"

The woman looked at her watch. "Another couple minutes," she said. "The next tour start in ten. You wanna ticket?"

"No, thanks," Alex said, and walked away. Making sure no one saw her, she made her way around to the back of the house.

When she got there, she evaluated her options, knowing the clock was running. She found a back door with a sign above that said EMERGENCY EXIT. *Right*, she thought—an emergency exit at a haunted house—but she was glad it was there.

Nearby she found a window with a shade pulled down. She went over to it and, using her powers, lifted the shade just a bit so she could get a look inside the house.

As soon as she could see in, it brought back vivid memories of her visit there. There were three rooms: The tour started out front in the living room, where there were some overstuffed couches and wooden coffee tables; the next room was the infamous dining room and kitchen, with a fully set table for two; farther back was the Harrison bedroom.

Alex checked around and, seeing that she was in the clear, concentrated and morphed into liquid form. The process of liquefying was exhausting, especially when doing it twice within a few minutes, but she knew this was the last chance to save herself, and her energy was high. She slipped through the crack at the bottom of the emergency exit door and found herself in the Harrison bedroom.

The room was filled with two small beds and some dusty bookshelves, but empty of people. From her liquid point of view, she could see the legs of the tour group moving forward toward the front door, obviously preparing to leave. At the back of the line she could clearly see the feet of

Tad and Tommy. She hurried to a corner of the bedroom and reformed. She then removed her boots, so that her steps couldn't be heard on the hardwood floors.

She walked carefully through the bedroom and into the dining room. She hid behind the doorway and saw the tour guide stop at the front door, facing the group in the living room.

"As you can see," the guide said, "a lot of people still feel that Alfred and Cecilia Harrison, despite their deaths, are still here, keeping a vigilant watch over their beloved home."

"What a joke," Alex heard Tommy say.

"Yeah," Tad added mischievously. "We were *real* scared." The twins laughed and nudged each other. Alex could tell from the looks on their faces that the group and the guide couldn't wait to be finished with these two wildcats. The guide opened the door.

"Thank you all for coming," she said. "Please come again . . . if you dare." The group started out the door.

Alex was ready.

She focused on the couch, spotted a pillow, and using her powers, deftly sent it flying through the air, dropping it at Tad's feet. He tripped over it.

"Just a second, Tommy," he said.

Tommy stopped. "Get up, Tad," he said as the rest of the group exited the house.

Alex then concentrated on the front door—she slammed it shut with a bang! The twins, now alone in the house, looked up.

"What's this?" Tommy asked, walking toward the door. He pulled on it, but his strength was no match for Alex's powers. "It's locked," he told his brother.

"What do you mean, 'it's locked'?" Tad said and went to help his brother. The couch, from the other side of the room, suddenly slid across the floor and toward them.

"Look out!" Tommy yelled. They both dived out of the way of the rumbling furniture, which stopped in front of the door, right under the knob.

"What's going on?" Tad said nervously. Alex could finally hear a hint of fear in his voice.

"I don't know," Tommy said. Alex then focused on a light fixture hanging from the ceiling. She zapped it. Throughout the house, all the lights began to flicker, creating a strange and eerie effect. Tad and Tommy looked at each other, then rushed back toward the door.

When they got to the couch, Alex concentrated on their backs, managing to pull them both away from the door and into two chairs. They tried as hard as they could to move forward, but the chairs started to slide backward along the floor toward the dining room. The boys started screaming.

"What's going on?" Tommy yelled. "We gotta get out of here!"

As soon as the words were out of his mouth, Alex took her plan to the next level. Continuing to pull them in the chairs, she backed up into the bedroom, hiding behind the doorway, still keeping her focus on their backs. When they were in the dining room, Alex turned her telekinesis on the cabinets, opening the doors, and sending cups, glasses, and dishes flying around the room. Still in the chairs, Tommy and Tad watched this display, their mouths dropping open in shock, until Tommy stood and grabbed his brother.

"Come on!" he yelled. "Let's go!"

They both ran back for the door to the living room, but as they got close, Alex closed that one, too. Tad tried to open it, but it wouldn't budge, either. The twins stopped and looked at each other, while Alex continued to hide in the bedroom.

Next, she stuck her head back out and focused on the boys together, lifting them both off the floor. She sent them around the room, their little feet dangling just a foot or two off the floor. She had to keep herself from laughing—they looked so funny floating around the room. Their legs were flailing and their mouths were open as if to scream, but nothing was coming out.

After a couple of times around the room, she gently dropped them both onto the top of the dining room table. For a second they paused, looking at each other in fear. Alex then dragged them slowly down the length of the long table, sending more dishes and silverware flying off into the air. They screamed, covering their eyes, as Alex sent more stuff spilling out of the cabinets. The twins were frozen in fear—no one had ever been more convinced that the Harrison House was indeed haunted!

Suddenly Alex could hear some muffled banging coming from the front of the house—people were trying to get in, but the couch was preventing them.

She didn't have much time—she had to complete the job quickly.

While Tad and Tommy sat on the table, their eyes closed, holding on to each other, Alex first flew all the glasses and plates back where they belonged. Then she closed the door to the bedroom, turned around, grabbed her boots, and slipped out the back window.

She waited outside about ten seconds, putting

her boots back on, then went back in. She ran ahead to the door separating the bedroom from the dining room, and dramatically threw it open. She found them in the same position as she had left them, too frightened to move. They were wailing.

"Tad? Tommy? Are you here?" she asked.

They turned to her. "Alex! Help!"

"Finally!" she exclaimed.

She ran to the floor, helping them up. "This way," she said. "Come on!" Holding their hands, she led them through the bedroom and to the back door. She dramatically kicked it open, setting off an alarm, and the three of them exited back onto the park grounds. As they got outside, they were met by a group of Luna Park employees, led by Mike, the nasty security guard.

"A-*ha!*" he cried, seeing Alex with the twins again. *"There* you are!" He marched over to Alex, grabbing her roughly. "You're coming with me, young lady."

"Leave her alone!" Tad said, pushing Mike. "She's with us!"

"I thought you guys said you never saw her before!" Mike answered.

"We were just playing!" Tommy said. "She's our sitter, and you'd better leave her alone!"

The guard looked at Alex, then at the twins, who

were pale and disheveled—and hanging on to Alex as if she were their favorite person in the world. "I want all three of you out of this park now," he said, "and I never want to see any of you here ever again."

"We promise," Alex said, turning to the boys. "You guys ready?" They nodded. "Let's get out of here."

They moved toward the main gate, the twins clinging tightly to her. They walked in silence, until Tommy looked up at her.

"Alex?" he said.

"Yeah?"

"Please don't tell anyone you saw us crying like that."

Alex looked down at their hopeful little faces. "I won't," she replied.

CHAPTER 10

The day had taken its toll on everyone. Annie and Ray were both exhausted from waiting nervously at the map for Alex, and by the time she returned with the twins, they were in a foul mood. Chris, Robyn, and Nicole had waited outside the park exit for a long time, before leaving the van and walking around front, so when they all got back to the minivan, there was a thirty-dollar parking ticket on the windshield. Alex had promised to pay for it, so combined with the money she owed for their park admissions, she was suddenly in debt way over her head.

Scott wasn't even there. According to Robyn, it

was getting late, and he'd promised his parents he'd be home in time for dinner. He had taken off, and Alex wasn't surprised—she knew the day's events had probably turned him off anyway.

"He said he was sorry," Robyn said weakly.

The twins? The twins said nothing. They just sat in the backseat, staring out the window on the ride home, their faces still red and stained with tears.

"I hope you guys are happy about running everybody's day and practically getting Alex arrested," Annie said.

The twins didn't answer, they just kept looking out the window. Alex thought she heard one of them sniffle.

"Leave them alone, Annie," Alex said.

"When the Watsons hear about everything that happened today," Annie replied, "you'll change *your* tune."

"I can't believe Scott bailed on you like that," Nicole added.

"Oh, come on, Nicole," Alex said. "We invited him to a party, then cut the party short to go chasing after two seven-year-old—"

"Brats," Robyn interjected.

"*Kids*," Alex said. The twins remained silent, as if they weren't even listening. But for some weird reason, Alex felt like taking up for them. They'd been through a lot.

"You were doing great with Scott until all this happened," Nicole said.

"So what?" Alex answered, her frustration showing. "He's Jessica's boyfriend, and he's probably with her now. That's the way it should be."

"Right," Nicole responded, angry and sarcastic. "You really believe that."

"All I know," Ray said, "is that I spent two hours at Luna Park and didn't get to go on one ride or have one thing to eat."

"Except for that foot-long hot dog you were inhaling when we met up," Annie said.

"Except that," he agreed.

The minivan's first stop was Nicole's place, where she and Robyn stepped out in silence. As they walked down the path to the house, Alex got up from her seat. "Wait just a second, Chris?" she said, getting out.

"Hurry up, Alex," Annie said impatiently.

Alex caught up to her girlfriends at the door. "Listen," she began. "I just wanted to thank you for everything you guys did to try and get me and Scott together. It didn't exactly work out the way we wanted, but I'll never forget what you did for me."

"But we lost the twins," Robyn said, sounding guilty.

"They weren't your responsibility. They were mine." Alex responded. "I should have never left their house."

"What's going to happen to you?" Nicole asked.

"I don't care what happens to me, as long as nothing happens to my dad."

"What finally shut the twins up?" asked Robyn.

"Guess they couldn't handle the Haunted House," Alex said.

"Let's *go!*" Annie yelled from the van.

Alex hugged Robyn, then Nicole.

"I'm gonna be grounded for eternity," Alex told them. "Come visit me once in a while?"

"We're there," Robyn said.

"Wish I could help you clean up the party," Alex said, walking backward to the vehicle.

"Sure you do," Nicole called back, smiling.

Alex got in, and quickly the minivan was gone.

Chris next dropped Alex and the twins off at the Watson house. Alex was happy to see that their parents weren't home yet. "Thanks for helping me out," she said.

"You got it," Ray said.

"No problem," said Chris.

"Annie, please don't tell Mom and Dad what

happened," Alex said. "I'll tell them when I get home."

"Believe me, Alex," Annie responded, "this is one story I *don't* want to pass on to them."

As Tommy and Tad got out, Chris said, "Later, boys," but they remained silent.

Once inside the house, the twins ran directly up to their room and closed the door. Alex sat down on the couch and waited for their parents to return home. She considered doing a little studying, but was too nervous and tired from everything that had happened. Instead, she just sat there staring into space.

She thought about what she might say to the Watsons. How could she possibly explain the unbelievable events of the afternoon? Even if she opened with Tad and Tommy's horrible behavior (raiding the cookie jar, ignoring their mom's instructions, locking her out of the house), would that make up for what had taken place later? No way. She had left the house with them. She had taken them to a *party*.

She was in huge trouble.

Her father was unemployed.

She felt like crying, but no tears would come. For some reason, she just wanted to laugh. The whole day had been so ridiculous that it deserved laughter.

Alex sat on the couch like that for fifteen minutes, until she realized that the sun was going down and she was sitting in the living room in darkness. Still, she didn't have the strength to get up and turn on a light.

She heard a car pull up and, moments later, a key in the door. The Watsons were home. Alex's heart started racing. She stood up and flipped on the lights.

"We're home!" Marian Watson announced.

"Hi," Alex said, her voice cracking.

"How was everything?" Mrs. Watson asked.

"It was a very weird day."

"Was it? Are the boys okay?"

"They're fine," Alex assured her.

Stan Watson wasn't convinced. "Boys?" he yelled. Upstairs, the door opened and Tad and Tommy came running down.

"Daddy!" they yelled gleefully, running into his waiting arms.

"Alex tells us you had a very 'weird' day," their mom said. "Is this true?"

Tommy looked at Alex, then at his mom and dad. "Not really," he said innocently.

"It was really *boring*," Tad added.

"Boring," Mrs. Watson repeated.

"She wouldn't let us do *anything*," Tad continued. "She wouldn't even let us leave the house to play outside."

Alex was stunned; she couldn't even be sure she had heard him correctly.

"She didn't?" Mrs. Watson said. "Good for her. I'd have been very disappointed in her otherwise."

If you only knew, Alex thought. She looked at the twins, and she actually saw hints of smiles on their faces.

"Were there any problems, Alexandra?" Mr. Watson asked. Alex hesitated before answering.

"Nothing major," she said.

"It sounds as if everything went very, very well," Mrs. Watson concluded. "Boys? Do you think you'd like Alex to sit for you again?"

Alex wasn't sure what she wanted them to say.

"Sure," Tommy said.

"Maybe we should make her like the regular sitter or something," Tad added.

The Watsons both turned to Alex and smiled.

"That's quite a compliment coming from them," Stan Watson said. "We've had a little trouble keeping sitters."

"Really?" Alex said, turning to the twins. "I can't understand why." Looking at them, she could see that they had turned back into the smiling angels Alex had seen when she first walked into the house. They were definitely the craziest two children she would ever meet in her life. "Well," Alex said, "I'd better be going."

She walked to the door as Mr. Watson followed, reaching for his wallet. Alex turned back to the twins. "So long, boys," she said. Together, as if rehearsed, they stuck their tongues out at her. Alex stuck her tongue out at them, and they laughed with delight.

"Here you are," Stan Watson said, handing her money. "Your dad told me what a sweet, responsible girl you were. I'm happy to see that he wasn't exaggerating. I've added a little extra as a bonus for doing such a great job."

"Thank you," Alex said. Anything to help her pay her new debts was a big plus.

"We'll call you about next weekend," Mrs. Watson warned.

"Okay," Alex replied. *I'm busy*, she thought. *Whenever you call me again, I'm busy.*

She walked back into the street, feeling almost giddy. Ten minutes earlier she was sure that not only had she destroyed her entire life, but her family's as well. Now it was all over, like a bad dream.

Everything was back to the way it was when she had gotten out of bed that morning.

Alex felt a momentary stab of guilt that they had not told the Watsons the whole truth. But Tad and Tommy were safe. And so was her father's job. And—Alex promised herself—she would never, ever do anything that irresponsible again!

Alex smiled again. She had even made some progress with Scott, though that part of the day had ended in a pretty messy way.

Up the block she could see a young couple walking toward her. From a distance they looked familiar, and as they got closer, she knew why. It was Scott and Jessica, their arms around each other. Jessica was back in town, and everything was the same. Harsh reality had come back to slap Alex in the face.

As they passed, all Alex could offer was a weak "hi." Both Scott and Jessica mumbled "hi" in return, and continued on. Alex walked a few more feet, then stopped to look back at them.

Scott had his head turned around, too. He was looking at her, raising an eyebrow. *Is he asking about the twins?* she wondered. She just nodded in reply. He smiled, Alex smiled back, and Jessica didn't see any of it. He then turned back around. Alex stayed where she was, watching the two of them walk off into the last of the fading sunlight. Then, just before she turned back for home, she saw Scott secretly put his hand in the air, his palm toward Alex, clearly waving goodbye to her.

She laughed to herself. She had definitely made an impression on him, but she knew she'd have to be patient. Scott and Jessica turned the corner and were gone, just as Alex saw the sun go down over the horizon. The day was over.

It hadn't turned out so badly after all.

About the Author

Ken Lipman was born and raised in Manhattan and attended New York University, where he studied journalism. Ken is an accomplished playwright who has been produced in both New York and Los Angeles; his plays include *Rosetta Street*, *Eddie Quinn*, and *The Precipice*.

Ken is also the producer, co-creator, and head writer of the television show *The Secret World of Alex Mack*, for Lynch Entertainment, broadcast on Nickelodeon. Currently, Ken lives in Los Angeles with his wife, Carol, and his two aging cats, Rico and Pablo.

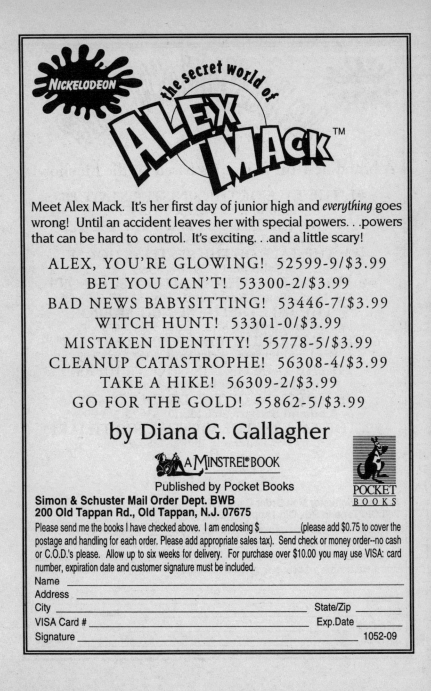

NICKELODEON

Are You Afraid of the Dark? ™

A brand new thriller series based on the hit show!